Fairywood Falls

By Steven Paul Watson

With many special thanks to...

My, loving wife, Sam, and her constant encouragement. To everyone who keeps pushing to pursue this wild idea that I can be a writer and pursue my dreams.

To Getcovers who took my vision of the cover and turned it in to something beyond my dreams. Immygrace who did a wonderful edit in cleaning up the stuff that I couldn't bring myself to change.

For my Grandmother,

Eula Boyd.

Works By Steven Paul Watson

Fairywood Falls

Howling Moon Series:
Howling Moon: The Beginning
Full Wolf Moon

Other Works:

Human 76 (Anthology Entry "The Hunted")

Table of Contents:

Prologue – Page 7

Chapter One – Page 15

Chapter Two – Page 29

Chapter Three – Page 47

Chapter Four – Page 54

Chapter Five – Page 66

Chapter Six – Page 77

Chapter Seven – Page 94

Chapter Eight - Page 110

Chapter Nine – Page 123

Chapter Ten – Page 129

Chapter Eleven – Page 138

Chapter Twelve – Page 157

Epilogue – Page 176

Prologue

It would have been the first frost of the year. Fall was so close now the tips of the leaves were beginning to change into more vibrant colors, but more importantly, she could feel the change in the air around her. It was a clear night, and it would have been the perfect morning, but still, there was no frost. The ground was cold to the touch, and steam lifted off the water in front of her, seemingly merging with the already-existent fog, making it hard to see the waterfall coming down into the stream no more than a jump away.

The sun started to rise in the distance, making the hills illuminate with those beautiful reds and oranges taking over the distant horizon. The air was full of moisture, and she could feel it as her soft purple wings fluttered, throwing the morning dew all about her exposed form, sending a tingle all over her body, raising goose flesh. The smile came naturally; this was her favorite time of the year. Soon there would be snow, and she loved nothing more than flying in the snow. She looked at her bare feet in the mud, squishing it between her exposed toes. Her naked skin glistened under the mist as she closed her eyes, feeling it splash against her face a bit harder now. An audible gasp from the slight breeze as it crept through the wilderness around her.

The wind carried with it a change of seasons, and it wouldn't be long before she would need warmth and clothing to get her through the nights. She took a deep, labored breath. Just the thought of having to go back to that house brought with it both good and bad memories. She couldn't remember what it was like before Mister Johnson took her in. She knew winters were rough and not quite the fun she had in them now. She often sat on lonely nights trying to remember what it was like before she knew not all humans were bad. It was a hard side of life to get used to, spending her youth believing humans were this vile species that would kill her if they were given the chance, only to realize they weren't. At least not all of them. The loss of Mister Johnson was almost more than she could handle sometimes, especially in the warmer months when she could hear hikers and campers nearby in the forest. She would sometimes creep through the trees to get a glance at them and listen to their conversations but couldn't make herself known to them. Once or twice she thought she had been seen, but if they had, they never spoke up. It was always there in the back of her mind; not all people were good. No matter how wonderful Mister Johnson had been to her, not everyone was going to be as nice to something that he called supernatural. There were times she had problems remembering Mister

Johnson's face now, and he had only been gone for what seemed like a minute. She remembered well those conversations on the back porch whenever it came up about introducing her to other humans. He always feared they would see her as something that needed to be dealt with. No matter how eagerly she wanted to meet and talk with others, he always convinced her it was not a good idea.

She stopped to ponder on it. She had lost count of the years it had been since he passed and frowned. It wasn't until she'd met Mister Johnson that she realized that humans kept their age by the year. In all that time before she met the old man, she never realized how fragile their lives were.

She had only been told to be wary of humans. They were dangerous, almost as dangerous as the beasts that would come hunt them at the changing of the seasons. She had never seen a beast herself, but her ancestors told her stories, unbelievable stories of mountainous-like creatures with monsters of an animal nature, not unlike a human's dog, who would come when the season turned cold. The things they said they did to the fairy folk sent a shiver of terror over her body.

Mister Johnson had said he saw one, one of the beasts that would come with the cold to hunt them. She wasn't sure if she believed him or not. It wouldn't have been like Mister Johnson to make up a story to try an frighten her but there were times even he said he was afraid he was keeping her from getting out in the world. He often had called himself selfish for keeping her a secret from all those who may have loved her as much as him. She had met him as a kid and got to see him grow old and pass. Even the thought of him made her eyes swell with tears. He had taught her so much about the world that she didn't know, the wonders of technology, and most of all, if it weren't for him, she would have never met Freckles and all the other wonderful dogs she had met. The wonderment of dogs and their impact on human lives and her own over the years. She smiled, thinking about Freckles and his half tail and how it used to wag when he got excited. She missed them both so much more than she would have thought possible. They had opened her eyes up to a world that she was taught to fear and avoid, and now she found herself missing the companionship they brought. She just missed having a conversation with someone, learning about the world around her that she could never be a part of. Maybe the loneliness made her so down and go back to his house and face the reality she was truly alone in this world. The tears began to flow freely now. She gritted her teeth, closing her eyes, wanting them to go away as they traveled down her cheeks. Feeling the mist on her skin, she forced a smile, listening to it patter off her flesh.

She took a long deep breath, trying to compose herself as she looked around the woods and then back to the water. The fog was beginning to clear, and she could see the small pond in front of her, and it warmed her heart. She took a couple of steps forward to the water, getting down on her bare knees and putting her hands in the icy cold blue depths. She swished her hand back and forth in the water, watching her fingers under the glassy cold surface. Her wings fluttered behind her, kicking the rain back onto the back of her neck, causing another shiver. She took a long deep breath before she splashed the water on her face. She wet her hands again, pulling her long white hair around and ringing it through, over and over until her hair was soaked and pulled neatly into a long tight ponytail around her neck. A few strands escaped and she pushed them back behind her pointed ears and again took deep breath. She glanced around at the place she called home. Mister Johnson had built the treehouse for her, a place she would be safer in than on the ground. He had built it so long ago that she didn't remember much about where she had slept before, just the cold darkness of the cave where she was raised. There was so much about her life before she took the chance with Mister Johnson that was lost memories to her now. He called it Fairywood Falls. She glanced back at the hand carved sign hanging at the base of the tree, it was one of the first human words he had taught her. Fairy.

She had not had a name before him, and he didn't like just calling her Angel, which he had from the moment they had met. He had settled on Nidaw, a word his grandmother had said meant fairy. An honest smile graced her lips, thinking about how he had pronounced the word Nidaw with his accent. A small laugh escaped her as she leaped into the air, letting the wind carry her, multiple wings flapping, lifting her several feet off the ground.

That's when she heard them. She was paying so little attention to her surroundings; they would have been on her before she could have formed a defense if she hadn't taken to the air when she had. The first coyote appeared through the underbrush looking at her, its tongue lapping out of his mouth. His eyes locked and narrowed, there was no doubt in what the beast wanted. It let out a slow growl bouncing on its front paws as it snarled its lips exposing blood-stained teeth. The coyote was angry, it also knew how close it was to catching her off guard. The coyote's fur was white and gray, and she recognized it. She knew this pack of animals well; she would go months without seeing them and then for weeks they would hound after her the winter months were the worst but at least then she spent most of her time enclosed in either the treehouse or Mister Johnson's old house. She grumbled under her breath, looking upward for a nearby tree limb to land.

The unmistakable sound of something cutting through the underbrush behind her. She didn't have to look for the second one. Just like the first, it made no attempt to hide its presence, letting out the low hum of a growl. She glanced back at him, the same angry look in its eyes as the first. It was the third and fourth coyotes that were the threat, they were there somewhere, she could smell their distinct scents now as they crept around in the unseen. She felt her wings begin to weaken, she would have to land somewhere and soon. This was how they took their prey, one or two would distract their target while the others would slip up on them to take them. Just the thought of how close they had come to her sent a chill down her back.

She sighed, unable to see the remaining beasts. It was another sign fall was coming if they were already starting to hunt her. She knew it would become an almost nightly occurrence now, when they were having trouble finding other game, they always came back to her. They'd run around the woods below with her scent on their nostrils hunting. Yelping out in frustration that they could never catch her on the ground. There would be nights to come she would not be able to sleep for their persistence. She looked around for the remaining two. She remembered watching the darker colored one try to climb a tree once after her scent, he wasn't to be seen now as she glanced over her shoulder at the reddish coyote lowered into a pouncing position. The darker one, he was the pack leader, the largest of the group, and he was sulking out there close enough she could feel his eyes on her, sending a chill over her.

This was the first time they'd caught her on the ground. Normally, they would have been in their den by now, but they must have traveled far in the night in search of food. By the whitish one's canines, they'd been successful. Maybe something bigger had pushed them from the den. More thoughts on the changing of the season and the stories of the beast crossed her mind, or maybe they had gotten smarter and waited on her this morning. She had been so busy enjoying the mist she hadn't even realized they were there. But now they saw the prey that had long eluded them. She exposed her own sharp canine teeth; she wouldn't be a helpless victim of their violence. She was no bunny rabbit or squirrel. Her wings would not carry her far, and she would have to do something about the coyotes.

<u>*Chapter One*</u>

Garrett

Growler let out a low bellow of a howl, causing Garrett Ware to glance over at the blue heeler puppy sitting anxiously at his side. He had barely moved from the passenger's seat through the entirety of the drive until he started to slow, and the animal was excited for the possibility of getting out of the truck for another walk. Garrett was just glad the dog didn't get car sick along the way.

"You okay?" he questioned giving the puppy a glance. The black and gray dog twisted his head to look at him, one eye was light blue, while the other was dark. He had the natural blue heeler colors that almost made the dog look blue, and he could tell by looking into the animal's eyes he was going to be a very intelligent dog. His biggest fear with the barely six-month-old pup was just how stubborn the animal would be.

"Yeah, you're okay." He ran a hand through his thick reddish beard. Gray was just beginning to take hold, giving it an odd blondish hue in certain light. He turned his attention back to the road in front of him.

Garrett looked to the rear-view mirror by habit, even though he knew he wouldn't see anything, and then glanced to his side mirrors to make sure the RV was still securely behind him as he pulled in off the main road. Hauling the RV wasn't something he was entirely comfortable with, and he had planned this trip down to every gas stop so he would not run into any turning issues along the few hours' drive.

He pulled far enough ahead so his wife could pull her truck off the main road with its attached horse trailer off the road securely. This was going to be a long day. Garrett hadn't prepared for how long it would take to drive in from Lexington, hauling along a camper and horse trailer on a windy late summer day. On a normal day, the drive would not have exceeded much over a couple of hours, but with traffic and the wind, it was already approaching noon.

He got out, taking up the for-sale realty sign from the front view of the road. He had hoped the realtor had already taken care of it, but considering the deal had just closed the day before, it was likely she hadn't had the time yet. He took another look around, still not quite sure what they were getting into.

Garrett glanced back, his wife still sitting in the driver's seat of her truck. She was busy looking at paperwork, or so he thought he could tell from the distance. Then he heard the growl of the pup in the driver's seat breaking him from his staring. He turned back, walking to the door.

The pup was looking at the old house. Garrett turned and took in the old house for a moment. In truth, when they settled on this land, the house wasn't of any interest to him. An old Victorian-style two-story with an old ten metal roof, long past needing repair. The windows all looked like they needed to be updated, and most of the siding was worn past salvable. He again glanced back toward his wife; she wasn't paying him any attention as he looked back at Growler whose hair stood on end as the puppy stared past him at the house, his legs bouncing with what Garrett imagined was a mix of excitement and fear.

Growler growled and let out a low bark as if he was seeing something that made him uneasy. Garrett glanced at the old house and saw nothing to be concerned about.

"It's all right, puppy. That's not our home," he said, getting a curious look from the puppy before it again settled into its spot in the passenger seat. He glanced back at his wife, her eyes were now on him, and he gave her a nod of recognition before he climbed back into the truck.

It wasn't far up to where they intended to park. It had been some concern on whether the road would handle the RV the entire way up to the clearing area that they had settled would be a good place for a small house and barn. He had put it into four-wheel drive just for this reason. He took it slow and steady the whole way until he parked. This was the move they needed. It had been a couple of years getting to this point. The hardest part had been finding the perfect property for their intentions to settle down and live a peaceful homesteader's life. It wasn't so much that they wanted to live entirely off the grid, but at least they could find some peace here. Here they could start a family. Life had not exactly agreed with them before. His wife had a miscarriage a couple of years before, and it had taken a lot out of her in the process. There was no way Garrett was going to take that risk again. It was part of why they wanted a farm. Once they settled in, they would once again talk about adoption and whether it would be a good choice.

"You ready for this?" He looked to Growler, but the question was aimed at himself.

He wasn't entirely sure if he was ever going to be ready for this drastic a change. The first thing he would have to get used too, living in the RV for the next few months or maybe longer. It wasn't exactly ideal. He picked the puppy up into his lap as he opened the door and stepped out. He set Growler down. The little pup was still bouncing and growling back in the direction of the house, even though he knew the dog couldn't see it. The house sat on a hill he could only see the outline in the trees, and he had to look closely.

"It's all right, Growler," he said.

He turned, going to level the RV in place and stake it out just in case strong winds came down into the valley. He looked at the trees around him. It didn't look like there had been many harsh winds, or at least there were no clear down falls caused by them. His next biggest concern was any trees that could possibly fall, but he saw none near enough that would cause any damage.

His wife pulled in beside him, not even giving him a second glance as she headed to the back of the horse trailer and started to remove their two horses. She tied them up nearby where fresh grass still grew, as well as some thorns for them to pick through on the side of the road.

After the trailer was leveled, Garrett went and started building the fire pit. It was all makeshift, and he wasn't sure exactly how easy it would be to find big enough rocks. Luckily the nearby creek had a lot to choose from to build the pit. He rolled around ten well-shaped rocks from the creek into a circle. Even now, it was well past midday, and he could feel the chill in the wind. It would be colder the coming night than the night before, and he just hoped it wouldn't rain. He didn't want to spend all their first night on his homestead hunkered down inside the camper due to the pouring rain.

He had hoped that they could at least have a small fire during the first night. He glanced over to his wife, who was busy brushing one of the horses, Jack, a solid black horse except for a white streak between its eyes. It was her horse, though if he were being honest, both horses were hers. The other horse to him was prettier, a painted horse with more colors than he could count named Max. He still had a fear of horses, so he didn't ride very often, and he couldn't lie to anyone; he couldn't keep up with his wife when they were riding. If Garrett were to be perfectly honest with himself, there weren't many areas where he felt he could truly keep up with her. Since the moment they had met he had always considered himself one of the luckiest men alive.

A rush of cold air ran up his back. He hadn't even realized he had broken a sweat, but the wind quickly informed him so. It was one of the regrets about moving in the fall; the nights were growing much colder in the evenings. Eastern Kentucky wans't known for frigid temperatures but there were still times were it would get colder, especially at night than would be comfortable to handle. Daylight hours would be working against them for the rest of winter until spring. He glanced at his watch. He hadn't realized he had spent so much time working on the fire pit. It was nearly four already and only a few hours until dark, and he needed to gather firewood.

"How are the horses?" he questioned as his wife circled around the side of the RV.

Naomi was wearing loose leg fitted jeans which still hugged to her backside in a way he couldn't stop himself from looking at her as she twisted away from him to pick something up off the ground. A pull over t-shirt and ballcap with her shoulder length blonde hair pulled back through the back of the cap in a ponytail. She smiled when she looked back at him, and he could feel his heart race. It had been obvious she had caught him looking and he gave her an appreciative wink for good measure.

"They're fine. How's the pup?" Naomi questioned.

"He's fine," he said, looking at the dog who ran and stood up on Naomi. "As you can see," Garrett gave out a grumble of his own. "That damn dog prefers you more than me."

"I know, I know it's supposed to be yours, but you know dogs, they have their own pick when it comes to people." She smiled, picking Growler up and scratching it behind his ear. He could see him wag its tail furiously before she put it back down.

"He's going to get too big to pick up like that soon," Garrett said with a slight growl of his own as she wrinkled her nose at him and placed Growler back down.

"You want me to start some dinner?" Naomi looked at her watch and back to him.

"No, we can have sandwiches and chips if it is okay with you," Garrett said as he turned back to fuss with trying to get a fire started. They were both from the area, if not exactly from the Virginia and

Kentucky border, where they intended to settle. But they had both been raised not an hour from the place they were now going to call home.

He leaned down, picked a small pile of kindling and brush up, throwing it into the circle of leaves and other kindling he had gathered. He looked up, and seeing his wife standing there watching him, she smiled, and he did the same as he stood and approached her. He gave her a kiss on the forehead and pulled her in tightly for a hug. "I love you," he said.

"I love you," she replied.

Garrett leaned in, kissing her again on the forehead.

"You going to miss living in the city?" she questioned.

He felt her grip on his side tighten. "Maybe," he said. It wasn't a lie. There were some parts of living in the city he was certainly going to miss.

"Me too," she replied, and he could feel her body tremble.

"Are you okay?" he questioned.

Naomi pulled away, and he looked down into her eyes. "Are we making the right decision?"

It was obvious to him, she was having the same second thoughts he was and the normal brightness of her eyes showed her fear. It was such a big decision to move back home where there was no certainty. Both took very drastic changes in their lives by retiring at such a young age, realizing they could have worked another fifteen or twenty years before they would have retired and lived comfortably. But they both wanted to do it while they could still enjoy life and were able to do so.

The horses neighed, and he could hear them stomping around in their position. "Are the horses going to be okay?"

"They will be fine for the night," she said, turning slightly to look back in the direction they were tied up. "I'll rope in a corral for them tomorrow around here," she said, making a motion with her hand. "And they'll be fine until we get something else formed. I'll ride each one every other day to get them to exercise. How about you? Where do we start?"

"Well, I figure I'll start on the east side tomorrow," he said, "start cutting a trail by the property markers that the county left for us and get a small field fenced in for them to roam free in until we can get the entirety of the property fenced next year or the one after."

"How many coyotes do you think are here?" she questioned. He hadn't really considered them. He poked at the fire, watching the sparks dance up into the sky before he turned and tossed a few more pieces of small brush on the young flame.

"I'm sure there's a few, but I doubt they'll bother the horses. Plus, we'll be here with them always. And that's why we have him." He pointed to the puppy. "When he gets a little bit older, but I think we need a second or a third one if we're going to expect him to keep them away."

"You just want a second or third one in hopes one of them will pick you." She laughed.

His wife was still looking at Growler when he glanced back at her. He ran a hand over her head, pulling the ball cap through her ponytail, and she smiled. Nothing made him happier than that one simple emotion on her face and a natural smile. There had been times he had wondered if it would ever come back to her. She smiled so much when they first met. And even now, there were times he knew the things that had happened to them still haunted her, but there were moments like this when he saw the happiness. He placed his hand on the back of her neck, the other on her hip as he pulled her close against him, her lips into his, and she welcomed him with a slight groan as her arms wrapped up tightly around his neck, pulling their bodies even tighter into one another. Her leg shifted where his hand rested on her hip, and he caught her there, pulling her upward, resting on his hips as she tightened her legs around him until he moaned under her pressure. He could feel the warmth coming off her, feeling her heart race sent the excitement running through him. Sometimes he forgot how long they had been together; he wouldn't admit it to her, but every day felt like they were still just falling in love to him.

"You want to know what would make me happy?" she said, and he watched as she bit down on her lip a moment before pulling away from him a little bit, looking up at the sky. She never released her pressure on his hips and continued to smile as Garrett took a moment to look up at the clear sky. "If we sleep under the stars tonight, it's the perfect night for it."

Garrett smiled, looking back at her, and then again kissed her, pulling her tightly against him. He could feel her there, safe and secure, as he took steps forward, one hand now resting on her lower back to balance her. "I love you," she said.

He looked up into her eyes, feeling her legs tighten around him once again, and for a moment, he thought he could cough under the pressure as he said, "I love you most."

#

They had their dinner and settled in. Garrett had a large fire burning in the center of the pit and was carefully placing other, bigger logs alone the edge so they would dry out from the heat. It also created a barrier for the fire so it would not spread unwanted out from its spot. He had settled on a location not far from the fire with a large cushion that was meant to go inside a mattress, and an air mattress on top of it.

He fixed a couple of sleeping bags which had been zipped together for warmth with a couple blankets thrown on top for extra heat. It was supposed to get moderately cold during the night but he knew with the thermal bags they were in no danger of freezing. It would give them even more reason to snuggle up together. His heart started racing the moment she stepped out of the RV, light from the fire dancing on her legs as she approached. She only wore one of his oversized t-shirts which had the sleeves cut off and then from the bottom of the arm hole most of the way down to the bottom of the shirt had been slit leaving it barely attached. He felt the excitement rush over him, she wasn't wearing anything else except an old pair of flip flops to protect her feet from the gravel drive. He couldn't help but admire his view as she threw a couple of small logs on the fire before she turned and smiled. "God, you're beautiful."

"Oh, honey, sweet talking will get you everywhere tonight," she said with a smile as she approached.

"Little guy going to be okay in there by himself?" Garrett questioned, not that he had wanted to try a change the subject. He had just lost his own thought process from the moment she exited the RV.

"He is the last thing that should be going through your mind at the moment," she said as she pulled up close to him. She was wearing lipstick, a dark shade of red that he could never remember seeing her wear before. Garrett wanted to kiss her, but she placed her hands up between them as he leaned in. She tugged at his shirt until it released and threw it somewhere out of sight. He didn't particularly care where she had thrown it. He watched as she tugged at his belt without mercy, and her forceful approach was turning him on more than he had expected. Naomi was aggressive in bed, not often, but there was a difference in her smile as she looked up into his eyes when the belt finally gave free. There was a feral intensity as she glared up at him with upturned eyes. Her lips turned into a mischievous smile as she tossed the leather strap up around his neck, sliding it back passed the metal buckle. Garrett felt himself gasp almost uncontrollably as he felt it against his neck, and she threw herself against him as she kissed him. He wrapped his arms around her, pulling her into him tightly. He could feel the one hand on his back still holding the end of the belt as she forcefully pushed her free hand down his pants. She worked her hand back and forth onto him until he growled slightly in her ear, and at once, she pulled on the belt, Garrett's head fell back, and he felt his jeans fall from his hips. Garrett released his grip on her body and placed one on the back of her head, taking a hand full of hair and forcing her to look up into his eyes. He was endlessly turned on by the wild expression he had never seen from her before. He smiled. Naomi pushed him with more force than he thought possible as he fell backward onto the makeshift bed. He laid there watching her as she approached, slowly one knee at a time until she was straddling his waist. He rose, meeting her halfway for a kiss. She smiled and he felt his own heart begin to race as she bit down on his lower lip. He loved this woman with every fiber of his being as he felt her bite down harder and and released a guttural growl.

<u>*Chapter Two*</u>

Garrett

Garret woke. Naomi's arm was stretched out across him. He rose slightly to look over at her, careful to make sure she was still asleep. He slowly shifted out from under her arm, she huffed in her sleep the moment he was free from her, even unconscious she knew he was no longer there. He smiled as he rose and walked barefoot over to the dwindling fire. He lowered himself and poked at the ash with a small stick, causing sparks to float toward the stars. He glanced back at Naomi again and smiled. She had shifted in her sleep, pulling the single blanket up to her chin. He tossed a few pieces of small kindling onto the rising flames followed by a few of the bigger chunks that he had left for the morning. A breeze shifted through the trees and earie sound caught his attention, wind chimes clicking somewhere in the darkness. He hated that sound, his grandparents had wind chimes all over their porch when he was growing up and they always seem to sound so chaotic when the wind blew. He never understood what people saw in them, his grandmother had an fondness for them. He stood there listening to them, hidden out there in the darkness. Their symphony was almost unnerving, sending a chill up his back. It wasn't until the sound of the crackling fire broke him from his gaze did the sound seem to mellow and disappear.

He stretched a moment, unsure of the time before he went to retrieve his pants. A sharp stick caught his underfoot, causing him to dance on his remaining leg for a second before he slipped his fee into his aged sandals. He pulled his pants up over his waist and looked for his shirt and belt, and neither were anywhere to be seen. He sighed and laughed simultaneously. His wife was never opposed to rougher sex, but she had never been the one to unleash it on him the way she had the night before. Just the thought of it excited him, causing him to turn from her and look back in the direction of the RV.

He approached the RV slowly, running his hands through his hair, he needed coffee, but more importantly, he needed to check on the animals. It still wasn't daylight, but he knew it wasn't far off. The sky to the east was beginning to make a pink hue from the approaching sun. He smiled, glancing back at Naomi for just a moment. It wasn't going to be a cold morning, not by his standards, but he figured once his wife was awake, she would be. He stepped into the RV. Growler approached, wagging his rear end. Garrett sighed when he looked at the torn-up chew toy nearby.

"You and those sharp ass teeth." He smiled, lowering himself to scratch the pup behind the ear.

He quickly fixed the propane burner on the inside and placed the coffee percolator on it. It was a habit both had, preparing the coffee the night before, so it only had to boil the next morning it was a habit he had picked up from his father. He stepped outside the door letting Growler out to stretch his legs as well. He figured the toy didn't survive the night because Growler wasn't used to being alone. He glanced over to his wife, who seemed to not so much have moved a hair since she had pulled the blanket up to her chin. He crossed the small distance to the horses; he hadn't even thought about bringing along a light or even his phone. The darkness was so fleeting, it would be daylight in a matter of moments.

Both horses were standing at full attention, staring off into the darkness. He approached them with caution, he knew the animals could sense his own nervousness but it was part of who he was. Growler quickly let a small yelp of a bark, catching Garrett's attention. He was looking off in the same direction as the horses. Garrett took a moment to follow their gaze, but he could see nothing in the shadows of the trees. He turned back to the horses, grabbing a large scoop of feed down into the horse's bucket, but neither of the horses paid him any mind. They kept their undivided attention on the shadows.

"Come on, pup," he said, walking back in the direction of the RV but keeping an eye toward where the animals watched so intently.

By now, the woods around him were beginning to brighten, and he could see better, but still, he couldn't see what was bothering them so. Or if something was even bothering them, Growler was known to overreact, even at a ground squirrel. It could have been nothing more than a deer. What Garrett did see, he didn't like. Though they had only been there a day, there was already some buildup from their presence. He sighed. He would have to change his plans for the coming day. They needed a way to keep things neater. The decision to build up a couple of shelters went to the front of the list to help unclutter the RV and vehicles, not to mention the grounds around them.

He could also see how much wood they had used in just their first night, and it was almost half of what he had gathered the day before. He would have to be more resourceful with the wood he gathered. Oak and ash to help keep a longer fire. And also, there would have to be less waste on the burning. He checked on his wife, who was still asleep, before he returned to check on the coffee. It was just beginning to whistle when he walked in, and he quickly poured two cups.

He returned, sat by the fire, and waited for his wife to wake. He didn't have to wait long, hearing the dog grunt out in pleasure as he twisted to look back to see her scratching away at Growler's head.

"Good morning," she said.

"Morning, love," he said with a smile as he retrieved her Halloween-themed mug from the stump at his side and crossed over to her. He helped himself to a glance at the ruffled t-shirt she was still wearing as she took the coffee cup from his hand. She smiled a big smile when she realized what he was doing. He wouldn't mind if she wore that shirt every day.

Naomi pushed a few strands of tangled blonde hair from her face. "I think we broke the bed." He hadn't even realized it when he had gotten up earlier, but the air mattress was completely flat.

"I blame you." He took a sip of his coffee, not looking away from her.

"You weren't complaining last night," she quickly replied with a blush. She sipped at her coffee to hide her red cheeks. Naomi was naturally pale, and it was always easy to see when she blushed, which wasn't often, but maybe she also realized just how out of character the night before was for her.

"I will never complain," he leaned in, kissing her on the forehead. Her cheeks flushed even redder, and he could feel her hand resting on the rim of his jeans.

"You find your belt?" Her cheeks flushed a healthy crimson, looking like she'd spent all day out in the blistering sun.

"No," he replied.

Garrett dropped to one knee as he placed a hand on the back of her neck, pulling her the remaining distance until he could kiss her. Growler released a small jealous bark, trying to push his way between them. The young pup pushed and huffed until he was firmly between the two of them and released another small whining growl followed by a bark, causing both to laugh.

"Fierce little beast." Garrett released a growl of his own and ruffled the hair on the top of the dog's head. He tried to swat away Garrett's hand before looking up at Naomi. Garrett laughed as he stood back up. "Damn dog." He smiled before he retreated to a standing position, and Growler looked proud of his accomplishment.

Naomi looked from Growler to Garrett and smiled.

"Some change of plans for the day. I was going to start some fencing, but I believe I need to get us some shelters up for storage." Garrett looked around, and in the few moments he had been talking to his wife, it was now complete daylight. He sighed, realizing the daunting task ahead of them.

#

Garret started his day by finding a few nearby locust trees, cutting them down, and making a stack of posts. Once he had enough so that he could build an eight-by-eight shelter, he spent more than half the day framing together so it wouldn't move. He sank the posts far enough into the ground so that they would be strong. This wasn't a shelter, only a temporary fix for storage.

He then cut more firewood to do a few nights outside nearby trees that were all dead, still standing, letting them fall to the ground. At least there'd be some warmth, and he figured at least a couple of nights of keeping a small fire built, not like they had built the night before that had burned throughout the night. He hadn't slept much or heard any coyotes either, but that didn't mean they weren't in the territory. Locals had warned him on a social media group that coyotes and black bears were very well-populated in the region. The closer they got to the Breaks International Park, the more they would have to worry about them. He was worried about bears coming into the area and startling the horses. But most of all, he didn't want to lose Growler to the coyotes knowing they would see the defenseless puppy as easy prey. Growler had shown he was very skittish about new things, but he was afraid that he might see the coyotes were just some other dogs, and he wouldn't see them as predators. He hadn't realized it, but he had spent most of the day working on the shelter and cutting wood, and it would be dark soon.

He knew Naomi would be back from town soon, and he wanted to have dinner at least on by the time she got back. Though it wasn't homemade, he opened a few cans of vegetables, fried up some meat and onions, mixed in vegetable juice, a healthy dose of salt, red pepper and mixed it all together, letting it simmer on the stove before he went to start the night's fire.

#

Naomi

The Rusty Fork Café stood out among the rest of the establishments on the main street of Elkhorn City. It was like the entirety of the small town had recently gotten a face lift, everything was painted and cleaned, and visually everything looked new. There wasn't much to choose from in the small town either, with no red lights and only a couple of caution lights nearing what she assumed were the busiest intersections. A small pizza place, coffee shop, and the only fast-food restaurant she'd seen as she drove around was a sub shop. The old café stood out for two reasons: It sat on the corner across from a large elk statue, saying, "Welcome to Elkhorn City," and it was also older in appearance than all the other buildings around. It had apparently missed the facelift procedure the rest of the town had received.

Naomi pulled up to the counter, and at once a waitress looked her way, giving a nod indicating that she would be there in just a minute. Naomi looked around the café. It looked much older on the inside than it appeared on the outside. She imagined the old café had stories to tell. It looked almost the same as she would have thought it had looked forty years before when the place first opened. Naomi settled in, grabbed the nearby menu, and started to look it over. A bell chimed behind her, catching her off guard. She hadn't even realized that it the door had a chime when she walked in. Two burly men walked in, sitting at the counter both wearing full camouflage overalls and orange ball caps.

"You can wait on them first," Naomi said as the waitress approached. The waitress passed her by, and Naomi smiled as a large map for the Breaks International Park caught her attention. She knew they were close to the park. It was part of the reason they liked the property they had bought.

"Well, you're new here," the waitress said, stepping up to her crossing her arms, and leaning on the old rustic wood plank counter. Naomi realized at once the woman was glaring at the circular nose ring on her left nostril, it was tiny, and she had gotten it after a hard time in her life. "You a tourist passing through?"

"My husband and I just moved in not far from here, or we're working on moving in," she corrected herself, glancing down at the old rustic menu again.

"Ah, that's charming. It's always nice to have new people here," the waitress replied. She was a much older woman with graying hair, and it seemed almost like she had an old eighties perm. "This little city of ours could use some fresh blood. Keeps it lively. We get a lot of passersby and lookie-loos coming to play in the creeks or run through the mountains, but not many of them ever stick around."

"So, what's good here?" Naomi questioned, knowing she hadn't really paid attention to the menu and was just taking in the old-looking café.

"Well, if you like burgers and fries, we have some of the best around. Fries are home cut," the waitress stated.

"How are your milkshakes?" Naomi questioned, looking to the waitress and then back to the picture of the milkshake on the menu.

"I'd recommend the strawberry shake. We use fresh strawberries from a local farm," the waitress said with a smile and pointed in the direction of a stand of freshly wrapped strawberry baskets. "Maybe pick up a basket or two as well. They don't last long once people realize we have them."

"I'll take two of those shakes," Naomi replied, glancing back in the direction of the stand, almost feeling guilted into buying strawberries as well. "And a basket of strawberries." There was a moment of hesitation before she spoke again, "also a plain hamburger well done."

"Good choice," the waitress said.

Naomi watched as the waitress took down her order and turned back, pinning it on the nearby hook for the cooks.

She came back to the counter. "So, what brings you to Elkhorn City?"

"Well, actually, my husband and I are both from the area, well, closer to Pikeville for him and Whitesburg for me. We decided to move back here from Lexington," Naomi quickly replied.

"Ah. Do you have any children?" the woman questioned.

Naomi groaned and hoped it wasn't as audible as it felt. "No, we haven't had any luck in that area, but we've actually thought about adopting once we get settled in here," Naomi replied, trying to fight the growing sorrow in her stomach.

"While there's always foster kids out there in need of a good loving home," the waitress said with a large unforced smile leaning into the counter. The scent of greese and cleaning spray radiated off of the woman causing Naomi to lean back and take a better look around the café.

Naomi wanted nothing more but to change the subject as she looked at the nearby sign behind the woman of a sasquatch crossing and smiled. "Are you a believer?" the waitress questioned. Her tone had changed when she looked back at the sign. The waitress turned back with a large smile.

"I don't know, maybe," Naomi had never really thought about it.

"Well, you're moving into one of the top regions on the East Coast for Bigfoot sightings, all the way from the Breaks down to Norton, Virginia," she replied. "Though down there in Norton, they like to call it the Wood Booger." Naomi laughed, and the waitress also chuckled at the name.

"What about the Elkhorn Fairy?" she pointed to a small sillohette drawing that was no more than a stick figure with large butterfly wings coming off it.

"Last year a couple kayakers said they saw it and that was the best they could come up with when we asked them to draw it," she chuckled. "If you ask me, they may have had a little too much weed that morning and passed out in a flower patch and hallucinated when a butterfly got a little bit too close to their face."

"I don't think I've ever had weed make you that high," Naomi winked.

The waitress let out a belly laugh as she looked back to her. "Good point, I think I like you. Where exactly are you moving in too?"

"Our land is in Kentucky but along the border to Virginia," Naomi replied.

"Oh, good territory then. I know a lot of people who live out there. What do you do now?" she questioned.

"I'm a retired schoolteacher," the woman gave her a questioning glare. There was no doubt the woman was older than her and was judging her for her age now.

"You're awfully young to be retired," the woman said with a big jolly smile that made her look much older than she probably was.

"I'm not as young as you may think I am," Naomi quickly replied.

"All that clean living, maybe," the woman replied and again looked over at the nose ring and wondered what exactly the waitress was thinking. Maybe some retired hippie teacher, which caused Naomi to snort, getting a questionable look from the waitress.

"Well, if you change your mind, I hear the schools here are really looking for teachers, so maybe you could substitute," the woman said, gaining her composure.

"Maybe," Naomi replied. That was a possibility she had thought of herself. Maybe she could substitute on the side if she really got bored, but it would be a while before she would have to make such a decision.

Naomi watched as the waitress went to the counter, grabbed two plates, and returned them to the men who walked in after her.

"Your order should be up soon, sweetie," she said with another big-hearted smile. Naomi imagined the waitress always smiling, which was out of habit. Whether it was a real, sincere smile or not, Naomi couldn't tell. Naomi was also surprised as she approached her after handing off the other two orders, but she was most likely trying to figure out who the new people moving into the area were.

"What does your husband do? Is he a teacher as well?" She settled back into her position opposite Naomi.

"He used to sell insurance," the waitress frowned at her reply. "He's retired as well."

"How old is he?" the waitress questioned, and she let her smile slip a moment at her surprise that they were both retired.

"Forty-eight," she answered.

The waitress smiled. "Awesome to you both for retiring young." Again, Naomi glanced at the sasquatch sign near them. "You should be careful out there. There are probably one or two sightings a year." Naomi was trying to smirk, and if the waitress noticed, she didn't let on. The last thing Naomi wanted to do was offend the woman if she was really a believer.

"What are these?" Naomi pointed to the case nearest to her with little stones with etched crosses sitting inside.

"Those are fairy tears," the waitress stated, opening the case and getting a couple out. Naomi gave her a questioning look as she opened the palm of her hand for her to inspect. "I know what you're thinking," the woman said with a smile, dumping the small stones into Naomi's hand. "But those are not hand etched. They're found in the Appalachian Mountains from North Georgia all the way up into Virginia, and every once in a while, people around here will find them. It's rare though, they're not as common."

"That is so unique," Naomi studied the stones. They felt like natural stones, and she seemed to feel some type of energy coming off them, like they were heating up in her hand.

"There's an old folk story behind them, why they're called fairy tears. It seems that when Jesus died"—the woman grabbed the cross around her neck and even closed her eyes for a moment—"it seems that the fairies of Appalachia cried and that formed these little unique stones."

She let go of the cross as you stood straight as Naomi dumped them back into her hand. She watched as the waitress returned them back to their place in the display. The bell behind her rang again as a couple more people entered, and she realized just how busy the little café was. The bell behind the counter rang but Naomi looked to the stick figure drawing of a Fairy inside of what order was coming up.

"Honey, I think your order is finally up." She turned back, getting a brown bag that was stapled closed and another bag with a basket of strawberries.

Naomi smiled as she handed the money over. "Keep the change."

"Thank you," the waitress replied.

"And thank you for the information," Naomi gave another glance at the sign as she headed toward the door.

"You be safe out there, and God bless," the waitress said, walking to talk to the other patrons.

Naomi took a moment to look around the town. There wasn't a lot in Elkhorn City, but she noticed a few nearby people sitting at a trail leading down to the waterway. They were obviously tourists and hikers who were probably kayaking the nearby streams. She wondered if the tourists knew about the Bigfoot sightings. She figured it might have been one of the things that drew people to the area.

#

Garrett

Garrett stepped to check on the fire. It was one of the things that he would have in the cabin once it was built; a fireplace. There was so much old timber in the woods around them that it would be years before they'd have to worry about outsourcing any other wood. He heard Naomi as she pulled in behind the RV. She had a big smile on her face.

"What is it?" he questioned, watching her jump from the truck with bags in hand.

"We got some horse feed and some groceries and other essentials," she replied, approaching with almost a skip to her step.

"Is that it?" he continued to smile, watching her approach.

"What did you do today?" she questioned, obviously in an attempt to change the subject.

"I worked on the structure and tried to build up our stockpile of firewood. Felt like maybe it was getting a little cluttered. Tomorrow I will be starting on a temporary barn. I already started dinner."

Naomi approached, giving Garrett a quick hug, "Smells good. I brought you a milkshake. It's quite good."

"I'll need you to head back into town tomorrow. I need some metal for the shelter and maybe see if there is a local sawmill around somewhere, so we can start on the small barn."

Growler was growling and barking behind them, catching their attention. "He's been doing that most of the day." Growler was sitting just outside the RV, watching toward the old house. "One of us is going to have to go to that old house show that dog there is nothing to be afraid of."

"He probably saw a raccoon or opossum over that direction and is still searching for it," she replied. "I'll stop in there tomorrow or the next day, and we'll see what's in there."

Garrett noticed the paper bag in her other hand as he took the milkshake from hers. He watched as she opened it, pulled out a plain burger, and leaned forward. Of course the smell of the burger caught Growler's attention, and the puppy quickly ran to her side and got his treat. Naomi was smiling when she looked up at him and then stood. "What is it?" Garrett questioned.

"Did you know that we have moved into one of the premiere Bigfoot sighting areas on the East Coast?" Garrett watched her smile, and he could tell she was trying to hold back a laugh. "Also, apparently there is something out there known as the Elkhorn Fairy?"

<u>*Chapter Three*</u>

Garrett

Garrett sat beside the fire in a camping chair, poking at the flames. Sleep evaded him each time he tried. His wife and Growler were sound asleep inside the RV. He had left them both sleeping comfortably. He did not want to risk waking them with his rustling around inside the small space. He sat back in the chair, looking up at the stars. Everything was playing out in his mind. Were they making the right decision to retire at such an early age and move out into the middle of nowhere? He was trying to reassure himself of their life-altering decision. There were so many options laid out in front of him. All those doors seemed to have closed the moment they moved back to rural Kentucky.

He heard a coyote yelp off in the distance sending a cold chill up his back. It was the first one he had heard. And if there was anything he knew, where there was one coyote, there were multiple ones. He looked to the pistol sitting on the stump at his side. Maybe they weren't as far away as it sounded. Without field cameras out there somewhere in the dark, there was no way of telling how close to camp anything was coming. He would have to get his wife to pick up a few cameras when she went into town. He grabbed the notebook at his side, jotting down the cameras in a long list of other things they needed. Not all of it was urgent, but by the time winter set in, it was going to get a lot harder to get things done with shortened hours and colder temperatures.

Garret heard something moving off in the opposite direction from the coyote yelp. He grabbed the gun and flashlight in one fluid motion as he stood, taking several steps in the direction of the new sound. He shined the light all around, stopping on any shadow he thought was something other than a tree. A large shadow caught his attention enough so he raised his gun, pointing it in the same direction.

"Hello?" he shrieked, sounding less threatening than he intended. He took a couple more steps forward, trying to hold the light steady, but a tremble had started, and the shining light made it clearer.

He could hear something move, walking through the trees and trying to be stealthy, but the mystery animal was too large to move silently through the dry undergrowth. Garrett's eyes settled on a spot that wasn't there before, standing near motionless, but he could see it as he slowly moved the light in its direction.

"This is private property," he huffed, sounding a bit more threatening than before as the shadows themselves seemed to move as the light lit up the area.

His mind and the darkness were playing tricks on him. He was so sure there was something there only a moment before. But if there had been something there, it stood on two legs and was larger than any man he had ever seen, and the stories his wife was telling him about the local Bigfoot myth caused him to smile. The lack of sleep was catching up with him now. He was almost convinced he had just seen a sasquatch in Eastern Kentucky. He huffed as he dropped his light, and again, the sound of something moving erupted, moving swiftly away from the light of his fire. Garrett moved a couple of steps forward, holding the light up again, trying to spot anything else in the darkness, but the sound was moving away from him now until there was nothing.

He tried to follow with his eyes the direction the creature moved but saw nothing. He took half a dozen steps forward, holding the pistol and the light up right in front of him.

"Get!" he yelled out, thinking about how massive the figure was. "Just a black bear," he mumbled mostly to himself, trying to be convincing. "Just coming in to investigate the potential new food supply." He sounded almost convinced about what he was saying. "Or…"

He looked back in the direction of the RV. He hadn't realized just how far into the wilderness he had moved. "Bigfoot." He laughed without meaning to, looking back in the direction the mysterious figure had traveled, thinking about how large it had seemed. But in the night, the shadows could play tricks on one's eyes. "It was a bear. It had to be a bear."

He let the hammer on the pistol fall back into a safe position. He returned to his chair, taking a moment to look back at the flattened air mattress where he and his wife had made love the night before, out in the open for everyone to see, and again, he snorted.

"Just a bear," he repeated, "coming in to investigate the new animals moved into its territory."

#

"We have company."

Garrett hadn't realized he'd fallen asleep as he sat up in his chair at the sound of his wife's voice. He looked at the pistol on the stump beside him and quickly covered it up with the notepad. Garrett tried to focus as he twisted to look back at Naomi. She had a pistol tucked into the back of her jeans, her hands forcefully resting on her hips as headlights approached from the mouth of the hollow. As it got close enough where the driver could see her, blue lights flashed, lighting up the darkness around them.

"I think it's a game warden," Naomi looked back at him.

Garrett retrieved his phone from the stump. It was flashing a bright red lighting symbol.

Naomi was fully dressed in jeans and a pullover t-shirt, and she was already in her work boots and her hair back in a neat ponytail. She'd been awake for a while.

Garrett watched as she approached the cab, and a man got out of the driver's seat. He couldn't quite make any of his features out or hear what they were saying. Garrett then realized there was a blanket wrapped around his ankles. Naomi had at some point covered him up and stoked the fire. He looked in the direction of where he had seen the mysterious figure hours before but could see nothing but the wilderness.

Naomi approached and smiled. She stopped when she reached the RV door and turned to watch the SUV turn before she opened the door.

Growler jumped out of the RV immediately and looked in the direction of the intruding vehicle as it spun its tires in the leaves. Garrett had not realized most blue heelers were wary of strangers until they got to know someone. They were very home-bodied animals.

"What did he want?" Garrett questioned once the vehicle's lights had disappeared into the darkness.

"Just thought we were someone trespassing. Well, apparently, from time to time, people come up in here and camp and hunt since the guy who owned the property died; he keeps a regular look. He thought he'd warn us. He also said there were bears in the area coming over from the Breaks park, but they were rarely anything to worry about," she said. "Mostly I think he was embarrassed that we weren't trespassers he could run off."

"I bet the horses won't much care for the bears," he said, looking at the two horses in the nearby freshly roped corral.

"Well, I've been planning," she said with a big smile as she approached.

Garrett sighed. "Of course you have. You've probably been up hours plotting out the grounds."

Naomi smiled. "Well, I'm thinking over there"—she pointed to a small cluster of pines—"that is where we can build a small barn just big enough for two horses, maybe some goats, some chickens just enough to eat, maybe four rooms, and a storage room." Garrett just shook his head yes. "And over there, we could build our cabin." She pointed not far from the small stream opposite where their camp was built. "I don't know, maybe what, three-bedroom one bath?" Naomi smiled. "Then maybe we can revisit the idea of adopting a kid." Garrett smiled at her. It was his intention; he hadn't gotten into the planning of the house. Apparently, she had.

"Then we need to get some lumber," he said with a smile, putting his hands on her hips and pulling her closer to him.

"Are you going to put some clothes on?" she questioned. Garrett hadn't even realized he was wearing nothing but a pair of sweatpants that he slept in.

"Maybe," he said with a laugh. "We're far enough up in here we might never have to wear clothes again."

"You would like that, wouldn't you?" she said with a laugh.

"Yeah, I'd like to see you not wearing another stitch of clothing. Maybe we'll turn this into our own nudist colony up in the mountains of Eastern Kentucky," he said. "I bet the neighbors would love that."

"Yeah, but I don't think the adoption agency would like that very much," she said, smiling.

"You're probably right about that, so we'd better take advantage of it while we can," he said, grabbing at her shirt, pulling it from her, and tossing it toward the broken air mattress.

Chapter Four

Garrett

The tree dropped, causing a scattering of limbs, leaves, and brush to whoosh through the woods. He set his saw down, looking at what he had achieved. There was a fence line four-foot-wide now spread out behind him. He had left smaller trees where he could, topping them off at six feet and set steel posts every eight feet to drive into the ground. He didn't look forward to the day he ran the wire, but at least he had made progress. The first time since they'd gotten here, he had done what he set out to do and was making better progress than he could have hoped. He never imagined all those years helping his father cut timber as a kid that using a chainsaw was that much work. He always thought it was just a simple cut and letting it fall. But now he knew better. He was soaked with sweat. He still wore his shirt, or he'd have been covered with wood shavings, and he didn't want that. His shoulders ached with every movement he made. He groaned as he removed his button-up flannel shirt and shook it into the air, knocking the sawdust to the wind. He ran his hand through his beard and hair, trying to get any excess that was there to scatter as well. After he thought he had gotten rid of most of the shavings, he removed his under shirt and repeated the procedures.

He took a long, hard, deep breath. He heard something off in the distance, what sounded like a tree falling. He looked in that direction. He imagined this was the sound that had been echoing from his whereabouts most of the day. But there was no wind moving. In truth, he would have thought it almost impossible for a tree to fall without assistance, given the perfect weather.

Something caught his eye in the distance, birds. They all scattered in his direction, circled, and headed back to where they came. Garrett smiled. The moment the birds saw him in their territory changed their trajectory and went back. He saw them fluttering through the trees, and something snapped a twig behind him. He turned, looking in the direction of his wife, but she was nowhere to be seen. The thought of the figure from the night before again came to mind. He had spent most of the morning trying to push it from his thoughts. His wife was somewhere on the horse he knew, despite his reservations about letting her go on her own, she was inspecting the border flags and putting up new no trespassing signs. He reached down and grabbed the bottle of water, pulling it to his lips. He was on his last water and hadn't packed anything for lunch. He hoped Naomi would come along soon with more. She was taking her time wherever she was at. He was doing the easy part, really, when it came time to set new posts and the fencing, which was when the real work would begin. The fence needed to be done by spring, when the vines and bushes again bloomed for the horses to eat. He also considered the goats that he knew his wife would bring in. Garrett hated goats; he really wasn't sure why but something about them always annoyed him a little.

He turned, looking at Growler. He was hidden away in the brush, watching him. Garrett smiled. Growler had also put in a hard day. Every time a tree would fall, he would run and investigate and then go back to his hiding spot safely behind Garrett. Garrett had just realized that he hadn't done it on this last tree.

"Hey boy, how are you doing?" he questioned with a smile.

Growler didn't come. Of course, the pup hadn't been happy getting stuck back, but the dog had a fear of horses, much like Garrett.

"Be that way," Garrett said.

Birds flew by his head, causing him to dunk at the sound going by. They seemed to be in lower and closer than you'd ever felt natural. "Wow," he said out loud. He turned to look back in the direction they had come. Again, another pod of birds had just flown overhead. It was early fall now, and he was sure it was only a matter of time before they'd fly south.

Garrett looked at his hand. He hadn't realized he was even bleeding. He grabbed the rag from his left pocket and padded the wound until the blood was all gone. He threw the rag to the ground not far from him. A bird flew by so close Garrett thought it had hit him in the leg, and then another bird flew through, grabbing the rag and packing it off into the wilderness. Before Garrett could react, Growler darted in the general direction till he was out of sight.

"Damn it," he said out loud. "Growler, get back here!" He had said it though there was no way he expected the puppy to listen.

Garrett quickly tossed the flannel shirt back on, then tucked the pistol back into its holster, grabbed the axe, and started to walk in the general direction where the puppy had gone.

"Damn it," he muttered again. This would derail his progress on the fence line.

He had walked straight in the direction the dog and bird had flown until he came across the rag that had been stolen. He plucked it from the limb. He looked back down at his hand; his knuckles where again soaked with blood. He walked to the nearby stream and sunk the rag into the cold water. He looked in the direction the water was coming from and wondered if a natural spring was nearby, something he would have to investigate further. He rinsed the rag out again. He tightened the rag around his bloodied hand and then looked around. He wasn't happy not seeing Growler nearby.

"Here, Growler!" he yelled out with his hand beside his mouth, trying to make his voice louder. He looked to the rag which was already soaked through with blood again as he grumbled to himself.

Outside of a crow, he had never seen any other type of bird pick something up and fly away with it like that, and these were small birds with black and orange feathers. He continued to look around, no sign of the puppy. Garrett whistled in the air and then clicked his tongue loud enough, hoping the dog would hear it and at least bark in response, but there was nothing. He looked down at the ground, and he could see his trail for something had run through, but surely it wouldn't have been a puppy; it was too evident a trail. But he decided to follow it anyway. The pup might have picked up a scent, and he himself decided to follow. He walked maybe twenty feet and found blood soaked into the leaves.

"Oh God," he said, his mind began to race. "Where you at, dog?"

Garrett whistled again, looking around for the little animal. "You've hurt yourself. Can you hear me? Where are you at?" Garrett paused for a moment as he ran a hand over his beard. "Bark, Growler, let me know where you are at!" he said in frustration. He was trying to control his breathing now, his heart thundering up in his throat. Anxiety was taking over; his wife would probably never forgive him if something happened to the dog. "Growler, where are you at?"

Garrett continued to walk through the forest. Keeping a hand not far from his revolver. As he walked the trail, it seemed to widen and grow more evident to him as he followed. He could see spots of blood shining in the light as he walked, making it easy to follow. There were leaves turned over in the path, making it easy and clearer to him that something bigger, much bigger than Growler, had come through. He walked and trailed, dunking under low-hanging limbs. As he followed, his heart continued to race. He wanted to continue to holler out, but the last thing wanted was for his wife to hear him and come rushing in, realizing he'd lost Growler.

"Come on, boy," he mumbled to himself, hoping he was all right. Before now, Growler had shown no courage to run this far away from them, and that bothered Garrett more than anything and made him feel that there was something wrong here. He just knew his wife was going to kill him if something happened to the puppy.

He followed the blood trail twenty more feet, coming alongside the stream again. He hadn't even realized he'd doubled back. His hands were not far from the revolver. Everything about this felt wrong now. He leaned down, ran his hand in the stream, and splashed his face, getting his hair and beard thoroughly wet. He hadn't realized he was sweating so hard. It didn't seem to be that hot, and he figured it had to do with the anxiety. He looked at his wounded hand. The blood was still staining the rag he had wrapped tightly around it. He took it off, rinsing the rag in the stream again before putting it back over his cut knuckles.

Snap.

Something on the opposite side of the hill broke out in a series of loud crashes, way too big, and made too much noise to be Growler. Garrett jumped the stream, pulling the revolver. He slinked through the wilderness, looking both ways to see what had made the noise or picked up its trail. He didn't see anything, no blood or anything that made the sound. He expected a large deer to break through the undergrowth or hear it snort off in the distance, or worse yet, see a bear's black shadow leaving the area. But still, there was that lingering thought of whatever it was that was in the camp the night before walking on two feet and larger than any bear.

"Here, Growler!" his voice went up another register, trying to call the dog out of hiding. It was becoming clearer that if he was close, he wasn't going to come out for him and that he might need his wife to come and call the dog before he would come out. He plucked the cellphone from the back pocket of his jeans, but instantly noticed he had no signal this far back in the hollow.

Snap.

Another limb broke somewhere nearby, but this time a large flock of the same birds he had seen earlier darted in and out of the trees coming in his direction. Garrett pulled his pistol and lowered into a crouching position, trying to make himself small to let the animals pass by. Something wasn't right with these birds here. He shifted in his position to make sure no others were darting toward him. He cleared his throat as he stood up.

"Here, puppy, puppy. It's time to head home to Momma!" All the time keeping his eyes on the nearby hill.

He took two steps backward away from the sound. He hadn't noticed it at first, a low humming growl, too low to be a canine of any sort. He gripped the pistol, holding it out in front of him, keeping his eyes in the direction of the rumble. Garrett took two more steps back and then a set of three steps before turning and heading back the way he had come, all the time looking over his shoulder for whatever had been growling. He stopped at the small stream again, looking at his hand. The blood was still coming from his busted knuckles. He reached down and quickly washed again, and he saw the blood trail on the other side of the stream that had not been there before. He took a moment to glance back the way he had come. There was nothing there following him that he could see. But he found he was having surprising issues with seeing stuff in the woods when he normally would with ease. Something was good at hiding in plain sight, and that didn't make him comfortable, especially with his wife somewhere out there in the woods. He stood, pulling the gun back from its holster as he walked alongside the stream and continued to do so for another twenty-foot, realizing he was back to where he had started. It bothered him that he had never once heard anything that could have been Growler. He was beyond a panic attack now. He was starting to face the reality that the puppy was gone. His frustration was growing with every step he took. He wasn't that far behind Growler when he went off after the bird and should have been able to find him with ease. "Where are you at, dog?" he said with a low growl of his own.

Garrett walked, always keeping his eyes on the ground, hoping to see some sight of Growler. He came to a fork in the small stream. You wouldn't think there was to be much water running out of the mountain, but there was, he had even realized that, but he was heading back toward camp and imagined one of these streams broke off into the creek by the road behind the RV. Garrett was at the edge of his own sanity, and all he could think about was how he was going to tell Naomi he had lost her dog. He gritted his teeth as he walked. He began to whistle, hoping it would grab the puppy's attention, but there was nothing. And that was even worse than nothing, but eerie silence swallowed everything, even the strange acting birds were nowhere to be seen. Squirrels, chipmunks, nothing... He didn't realize until now he hadn't seen any sign of any deer, no tracks, while they knew a few miles away that population of the whitetail was booming. Why was this holler so different? He rested his hands on his hips as he tried to catch his breath and control his breathing. He took several steps forward and quickly realized the birds were once again swooping through the treetops but not coming down into the woods themselves. It was almost as if they were following him or trying to warn him of something. The birds were really starting to creep him out. The wind shifted, and the sound of wind chimes echoed around him. He looked ahead, and it was easy to see the silver chimes hanging not far from him. He quickly stepped forward, grabbed them in a tight grip, and jerked them down out of the tree. The line holding them snapped instantly. He twisted the lines around the chimes tightly and stuck them at the base of a nearby tree to come back and get later.

Again, he started walking. He kept walking this time with a little bit more speed than before, the trail had gone cold again, but he was heading back toward camp, and for a moment, he wondered if Growler had gone back home. He stopped at the edge of a clearing, mostly looking for his wife and the horse. He heard whimpering coming from behind him. He quickly turned, pulling the revolver in the process and pointing it in the direction he had come. He thought about the low rumbling growl from the hour before, all the things walking that were always just out of sight, and even the shadow he had seen the night before in the wilderness.

Garrett smiled, seeing Growler standing only a couple of steps away, scratching at his ear.

"There you are," he said out loud as he rushed forward.

He picked the little dog up, inspected it, and found the bloody paw. It was coming from the padding underneath; he had cut himself, and Garrett couldn't help but realize the similarities to where he himself was cut.

"You shouldn't have run off like that," Garrett said, and Growler replied with a sad whimper. He tried to sound like he was disciplining the dog, but mostly, he was just happy to see he was back safely at his side. He inspected the paw closer, not being able to talk much about the wound, and he wondered what he had gotten cut on. "You look like you're going to need a stitch." He pulled the rag off his own hand and wrapped it around Growler's paw, and headed off in the direction of the RV. All the while, he continued to look for his wife and the horse, they wouldn't have been hard to miss, but the problem was she was still somewhere back in the hills.

Garrett took several steps forward. He hadn't even noticed the smell, and once he had, he started gagging. The musky smell of decay and death hung to the woods around him, causing him to hold Growler with one hand and pull the revolver with the other. Then he realized the smell was also coming from the dog he held tightly in his arms.

He started in the direction of the trailer. Picked up his pace, and they kept walking until he could see the trailer nearby. He saw all the horses tied up there. He knew his wife was there. That was both good and bad. He was glad she'd made it back home and was all right. Now he would have to explain how the puppy got hurt.

Chapter Five

Naomi

Naomi had ridden most of the perimeter, she had left Garrett shortly after daylight, and she figured she was somewhere on the west end of the property now. She had followed the red properties flags the entirety of the way. She saw the national park signs on the other side of the boundary from time to time, but it wasn't marked as clearly as she had hoped. She could plainly see a hiking trail or maybe a bicycle trail not far over the line. It was a worn trail, and she imagined that it saw traffic almost daily ever season except for maybe winter. She still wasn't sure just how bad the winter was expected to be in this part of the region.

Naomi kept going. She wanted to see just how far back their property went, she hadn't come with her husband when he surveyed the area, but she imagined that he didn't see all of it himself when he made the visit. She came to a small stream coming out of the National Park side of the property, and she followed it back into her region maybe a hundred feet, when she saw a large dig in the land itself down a small embankment before it started a steady slope again. She dismounted the horse and slowly approached. The water cut through the terrain and created a small pound maybe ten feet in diameter at the base of the embankment.

Naomi circled around until it was easier to lead the horse down the embankment. When she reached the bottom, she got a better look at the crystal-clear waterfall, which was no more than ten feet in height from where it started to the small pond below. The water formed a perfect silhouette of ledges as it traveled down the steep incline. It was easy to tell this was no man-made waterfall. This had been there, untouched for centuries.

Naomi stopped at the edge of the small pond letting the reigns of the horse go, and it stepped forward and started to drink. She wished she had her camera; the waterfall was so beautiful in its untouched beauty. She imagined if the park system had known the waterfall was there, they would have cannibalized it into its property long ago

Naomi sat down on a moss-covered rock at the edge and began to slip her boots off. She placed her socks inside and rolled up her pant legs to just below the knee. She took off her overshirt, tossed it beside her boots, and stepped into the water. It was cold. Ice cold, she stepped until the water was just under her rolled pants. She leaned down, splashing the cold water on her face. Naomi circled around and passed her horse until she was near enough to the waterfall to hold her hands out and catch the water. It was no warmer than where she was standing, but she smiled as she took a deep breath and two quick steps. The water surrounded her in an instance, though it didn't look like a lot from outside. It was only a moment before the entirety of her t-shirt was soaked and her pants as well. She started breathing heavily as she pushed the hair back out of her eyes, and then she saw the old oak tree on the opposite side of the pool. The old oak tree roots were exposed, causing a cave to form inside the mountain. She imagined once upon a time, a flood had pushed its way into the soft dirt around the oak's roots and hollowed it out. She crossed the stream slowly to step inside, the thought of it being the perfect hideaway for a small black bear caused her to glance down at the mud just around the roots, but there were no visible tracks. The cave was only about four feet in width and almost equal in height, but it was too dark for her to have any idea of its depth.

Naomi looked to the ground below, seeing something shining in the water. She dropped to one knee and scooped her hand into the shallow pool. She saw the small stones with crosses etched into them, as well as several arrow heads and other shiny objects. She saw the crow land on a nearby limb, staring at her, its head twisting from one side to another, taking in what she was doing. She looked again at the water and dropped the small coins back in, and as she did, the crow took off swooping through the wilderness again. She sloshed her way around the edge of the pool until she was at her horse, dropping her treasure into the saddle bag.

She turned and ran her hand across the horse's mane, which was paying little attention to what she was doing.

"You ready to get out of here?" she questioned, returning to her shirt and putting it back on. As she pulled her head back through, she saw something peculiar, a ladder coming down from the thick oak all the way to the ground. She didn't put her boots back on as she carefully crossed the pool and went up the embankment to where the ladder was hanging down. On the tree at the base of the oak tree where the nearest rope clung was a hand made sign that said, 'Fairywood Falls'! Naomi turned and looked back at the water, someone had put the stones there for a reason and now the sign. She couldn't help but think about the Ekhorn Fairy drawing back in the small city and she let out an audible laugh before turning back to the hand made ladder.

She let her eyes follow the rope ladder upward, she saw where it went, and then she saw the painted black bridge heading over to another tree. She sighed. Apparently, the people who owned the property before them had built a tree house back there. Naomi jerked on the ladder, testing the ladder with her weight, she could hear it strain with her, but it still held without breaking. She wondered how long it had been since anyone had climbed up. She didn't have the healthiest appreciation for heights; she was terrified of them. She started climbing five, ten, then fifteen feet up in the air. She finally reached the platform, careful not to look back down where she had climbed. She could only imagine what Garrett would have said to her for taking such a risk. She pulled herself up and into a seated position. She took a long deep breath looking out across the bridge. She got up onto her feet, her legs shaking as she started across the wooden bridge, the small planks across the way with rope railing. Someone had taken their time to do this and had used well-preserved material for it to be as healthy as it was.

"This is stupid," she said out loud, but still, she took two steps out.

The bridge swung violently with her, but it was holding. She couldn't imagine how much damage it would do if it was to break and fall with her. There was also the thought of just how long it would be before Garrett would come looking for her. She sighed as she took two more steps forward and then two more. She kept the same routine, two steps at a time, until she crossed over the ten-foot bridge.

She was on another landing now with the small tree house. It wasn't a big building; ten by ten at the most was what she thought from looking at it from the outside. She still dared not to look down. She would have to cross back over this bridge and climb down.

She pushed the door slightly open, her heart racing as she stepped inside. She was amazed at what she found. There was a glass window to the left looking out in the direction of the National Park. She imagined from this point of view, someone could watch hikers as they passed by, but there was very little chance they could see the voyeur. She entered completely. A small bed, old white sheets, and blankets lay about the bed. They looked like they'd been washed recently. Someone had once upon a time spent a lot of their free time here. There were a dozen or so books, beaten and warn with age and exposure to weather, but still good enough. When she opened the first page of the one on the table, it was readable. Naomi took a moment to look around. There were more than just books. There were art pads, notebooks, pencils, and pens everywhere you could see now that she was getting a closer look. Naomi smiled. It almost looked like a writer's retreat to her. A small one-person hammock with many of the tethers torn apart already hanging just above the books. Obviously, this is where someone sat looking out the window while reading, writing, or drawing. It was beautiful and well-taken care, which sent an uneasy feeling about her, it had been years since the last landowner died, but looking at the sheets, someone had been in the tree house in the past few weeks. Maybe some hikers from the nearby park had discovered the treehouse and from time to time used it as their own little getaway.

Naomi looked back at the door. "Hello?" she muttered, feeling she was being watched.

Naomi shrugged as if to push it all out of her mind. This was hers and her husband's now. Maybe she would make Garrett fix up the bridge and the ladder so she could come back here and enjoy her time away. It would be a retreat, and it was exactly what she needed. She stepped back out onto the little platform waiting before she started across the bridge again. She could see another structure in the distance, maybe fifty feet away, back onto the property a little further. She saw a little well and another structure. It was like a little community underneath her that she hadn't even realized until she'd gotten high above the rest of it. She smiled, wishing again she had brought her camera with her; it was rugged and overtaken by nature but still beautiful to her.

Naomi made her way back across the rickety bridge and down the ladder. First, she went to the old well. It wasn't far from where she had left her horse. She could see the horse clearly from the well, still enjoying its time by the small pool. A small wooden bridge, like the one she had crossed overhead. She walked across the top, but this was all wood made in the small planks of a cut tree. There were several rotten spots on this bridge. If the one up top had been this one, she wouldn't have crossed it. She reached the well, the rope splintered and broken at the top, and then she wondered if a bucket was at the bottom of the dark tunnel.

"Hello?" she said, listening to her voice echo back at her. She picked up a small rock pebble, just enough to make a splash, and dropped it down in the well. She counted to almost fifteen before she heard the splash coming from the bottom. It made a hollow-like gulp on impact. She knew it was deep. Maybe they could replace the rope and drop a bucket down and have the water tested. She hadn't noticed them before. Maybe the wind wasn't blowing. Chimes chirped and echoed from a nearby limb. She approached and stopped them for a moment and smiled. She knew Garrett hated them, but it always brought back found memories of her childhood home. Maybe that was the biggest difference between the two of them. She had as close to a perfect childhood as she could have hoped growing up in Eastern Kentucky. Surrounded by a loving family, though money was rough at times, there was always food on their plates, and she remembered most fondly the nights on her grandparents' back porch when most of the extended family would gather on the weekends to play music. And the wind chimes always seemed to mix in with the music almost to perfection. Garrett had a much different childhood, though the same situations, but he had an alcoholic, abusive mother, and often times he was left on his grandparent's porch so she could go off and party. She knew he didn't like to talk about it often.

Naomi turned to look in the direction of the remaining structure she had seen from the treehouse. At a distance, this building looked much less appealing and almost sinister in its appearance. She hearts a tree fall in the distance; it had been some time since she had heard any falling. And long before she had stopped hearing Garrett using the saw, maybe she had circled back around further to camp than she had even realized. She glanced back to make sure the horse was still happy with its spot by the watering hole. She wasn't going to walk the other building without her boots. She quickly returned to the horse and put her boots on, and grabbed her cell phone from its place in the saddle bag. There was no service, but it was the closest thing she had to a flashlight. She turned to look back in the direction of the shack, she could barely make its outline from the pool, and it looked even less inviting from where she was now standing. Naomi sighed, grabbing her pistol from her saddle bag as well and tucking the holster onto her belt.

Naomi approached the old wooden shack with more caution than the treehouse. It could have easily had something on the inside waiting with it being on the ground. But it wasn't just that; its appearance gave her a chill of terror. She was still debating whether she should go in and check it out alone. It left a much more unsettling feeling in her stomach as she stood looking over it. When she started toward it, a snap of a limb caught her attention. She turned to look in the direction she thought it was but saw nothing. She took a deep breath, and a foul odor of something dead caught her; she hadn't smelled this from the tree house. She urged herself to take the remaining steps until she was close enough to get a better look at the shack. She pulled the pistol in the process. There was no doorknob, just a hole for her to place her hand in and pull. She figured it was a hunting cabin of some sort, but she saw no way for a hunter to see or shoot from the inside. She kept going putting her hand in the slot, and slowly began to pull it open. The door wanted to fall off the old metal hinges. She stepped inside. It wasn't a big building, but every corner seemed to cling to shadows. It was even smaller than the tree house. Everything about this building made her feel ill as she breathed it in. She placed a cloth over her mouth, trying not to gag. She shined the flashlight and shot it around. The ground itself was wet, even though it hadn't rained in days. There was no reason for the ground to still be this wet. It was almost as though something had been slaughtered there.

She kicked her foot up to look at the bottom, a mix of mud wetness and crimson blood. It made her wonder how something so vile-smelling and eerie could be so close to the treehouse that was so beautiful. She stepped out of the building, looking for anything that could have been the source of the smell and blood, but she saw nothing. Even the ground on the outside of the cabin was clean of it. The smell was so bad it was taking her breath away. Naomi quickly went to the horse and mounted up.

Chapter Six

Garrett

Garrett filled a small tub with warm soapy water, and they washed Growler when he got him into camp and cleaned his foot. Naomi had finished bandaging Growler's foot when he came back into the RV. He was happy the smell was gone. Garrett had wanted to go back and try and find the origin of the smell the young dog had gotten into, but by the time he was cleaned and bandaged up, the last thing he thought he should do would go trampling around the woods in the dark. He had told his wife about the sounds he'd been hearing and how strangely the birds had been acting. Naomi had told him about the waterfall, the treehouse, but most importantly, what seemed like a butcher's room on the other end of the property.

"You say you could smell something dead on the other end of the property as well?" Garrett questioned as he washed his hands for the fifth time since getting into camp.

"Just like whatever Growler got into," Naomi was washing her hands again as well. Even though the puppy smelled better, the horrendous smell was stuck to them.

"I'll go out and investigate it tomorrow. We were a long way away from the back of the property. No way he got into whatever you were smelling," Garrett said, stepping closer to her.

Naomi took a quick step back away from him, and her hand went directly to her mouth. "You stink." She laughed.

Garrett had tried not to smell himself, but he knew he had gotten some of whatever it was on his clothing when he picked Growler up. "I'll let the water warm and jump in the shower," he said, giving a glance back to the shower. There was barely enough for one person to fit in the cramped RV shower. "You want to join me?" He gave a hearty smile.

"And break the shower like we did the air mattress?" Naomi winked at him.

"We can try." He laughed, looking at the bowl on the table nearby. He dropped his hand into the bowl, looking at the assortment of rocks and old arrow tips.

"I wanted to show you what I found today before all of the excitement," Naomi said, coming to the side of the table and looking down at the bowl. Garrett had once again fallen into his earlier thought as she leaned forward. Naomi was wearing a white tank top without a bra and still wet from bathing Growler. Naomi quickly noticed him looking. He smiled, placing a hand on his jaw, and turned his attention back to the bowl. "Not until after you shower." She dove her hand into the bowl, plucking out a couple of the stones. "I found fairy tears," she said with astonishment in her voice.

Garrett plucked one of his own from the bowl. "What are they?" He would have admitted he was amazed by how well-preserved the arrow tips rather than the stones.

"Fairy tears. They say when Jesus died, the fairies of Appalachia shed tears, and those tears turned into these old stones. But for the most part, these normally were only found in the Appalachian Mountains part of Southern Virginia and Northern Georgia but never Kentucky."

"I had never heard of these," Garrett said with his own amazement.

"Honestly," Naomi said while sticking her tongue out a little, "I hope I sounded like I knew what I was talking about. But the other day over at the Rusty Fork Café, the waitress was telling me about them, and I googled them after I got home that night."

Garrett smiled. "You had me fooled. Thought you learned about them in school."

"Now, go get that shower," Naomi said, crossing her arms against her chest, "I fully intend on using you after you are done."

#

Garrett was awake before the alarm, not that he truly slept during the night. He kept running the events of the past few days through his mind, the mysterious animal walking on two legs, the sound of something growling and something decaying somewhere nearby, but they couldn't find anything dead. He checked on Naomi, who was nested under a thick blanket, and he knew somewhere around her feet, he could see the mound of Growler tucked away in the covers.

"Good dog," he muttered, seeing the mound move slightly. He gave the puppy a pat through the blanket before he pulled his sweatshirt and pants on and stepped to the door.

He had an uneasy feeling running through his stomach, the feeling of being watched. Garrett glanced back at the window nearest the bed where his wife lay, but the curtains covered the entirety of the window, and there was no way anyone or anything was peeking in. He slides the curtains at the door open for a moment to look out. The fire was mostly just hot ash now. He had gone against his new rule of not over stacking the fire at night for the second night in a row. He had hoped there would still be flames when he woke. He shut off the alarm on his cellphone as he stepped out into the cold morning air, it still wasn't daylight, but he knew he had a full day ahead of him. He walked to the fire, picked up a couple of mostly dry pieces of wood, and tossed them onto the hot ash. He heard the instant sizzle from the hot ash as it started. A smile graced his lips. Picking up the stick he had chosen to use to poke at the ash and giving it three quick stabs, sparks flew up into the air, and a small flame kicked up between the two pieces of wood.

Smack.

Smack.

Smack.

Garrett almost didn't hear it; he probably wouldn't have paid any attention to it if it hadn't been so quick in repetition. The sound of something large being slammed into the side of a tree nearby, as if someone was practicing their swing with a baseball bat. Garrett stepped away from the fire. His hand went to his hip where the pistol normally would have been before he realized he had left it inside on the kitchen counter.

Smack.

Smack.

Smack.

Garrett lowered himself into a crouching position. This time, the sound was much closer than the last. He picked up the axe from the ground at the wood pile and stood. Three quick steps back to the fire, he used his off hand to again stab at the fire and sparks erupted into the night air around him. He lowered himself again, throwing a couple more pieces onto the fire, and stood.

Smack.

Smack.

Smack.

Even closer this time than the last, he glanced back at the RV, and for a moment, he thought of rushing for his gun.

"Hey!" he yelled out into the darkness. His grip on the axe tightened, and a cold chill raced up his back. He could feel it, that eerie feeling again. Undoubtedly, whatever was making the sound was looking directly at him. He used to never be so cautious, but the past couple of nights had started him rethinking a lot of things.

"You okay?" He quickly raised his hand. He hadn't heard the door to the RV open, but his wife's voice seemed to carry on the air around him. It was only a moment after she had spoken. She was standing by his side. "Are you okay?"

"Shh," he gave a small hiss waiting to see if the smacking sound would continue.

The two of them glanced at one another before looking back out at the darkness. His grip on the axe tightened, and he heard the hammer of a pistol being pulled back. Naomi had not forgotten her gun. After what felt like five minutes, he turned and looked at her. "I thought I heard something."

"What was it?" She turned and looked out toward the darkness with him.

Garrett smiled. He was glad she never questioned his sanity, not that he wasn't already questioning it himself. "Three consecutive smacks on a nearby tree, as if someone was taking a thick branch and hitting it, all times out and maintained, happened three times." He didn't have to ask her if she believed him. He could hear it in her breathing as she felt her lean in close to him. "Whatever it is, I think it's gone now."

"Let's go back to bed," Naomi stated. "Let's go back to bed and sleep in this morning, we'll have ourselves a good breakfast, and we'll go out and see if we can find whatever it is that is dead on our land."

Garrett smiled, tossing the axe back to the ground. He let Naomi lead the way back to the RV. They reached the door. They both turned and looked back in the direction of the fire and then at each other. Naomi started to step inside, and Garrett grabbed her arm, turning her back toward him. She was already standing on the step by the time he reacted, and he caught her around the waist, leaning into her until he positioned her back against the RV. He felt her legs wrap around his hips as he looked up into her eyes and smiled.

#

Garrett woke and rolled over, looking at the curtain leading to the outside. He slowly picked the corner up and peeked out. It was daylight, and the sun was shining brightly. He could smell bacon and hear it sizzling on the nearby stove. He rose, and his wife was completely dressed. He kicked the covers off, shifting his legs off the bed. Growler came over, sitting beside him, but even he could tell the dog was more interested in the bacon. "Any coffee?" he questioned.

Naomi walked over to the table, setting the coffee down. "You look prepared this morning," he took it in hand and took a quick sip.

"It's almost noon," Naomi said, scratching Growler on the head. "I went out and got a couple came cameras. Too much going on out there that we're not seeing. Paid a little more than I might have wanted, but the hardware store cut me a deal buying two. I've only been back long enough to get dressed and start breakfast."

"Did you sleep any after we came back in?" Garrett questioned.

"No," she replied. "After you fell asleep I ended up opening the window and just listening until it was finally daylight."

Garrett got up and plucked a worn pair of jeans from the corner and pulled them on. He finished latching his belt and grabbed another sip of coffee. "We leave Growler here today. We'll go out and see if we can find the source of the smell. "

"Horses?" she questioned.

"Preferably not. We should be able to walk the entirety of where Growler got separated from me yesterday and find it. As foul as it smelled, you would think it would be easy to find," Garret said as he grabbed at the sandwich and started to eat.

#

Garrett checked the revolver to ensure each cartridge was loaded, and he had the 30/30 rifle strapped to his back. He glanced back to his wife, who had a pistol on her hip as well. They'd both put on snake leggings. Though the nights were getting colder, it was still rattlesnake country, and they wanted to the extra precautions since they would be going through more brush piles. He led the way back to the stream where he had found Growler the evening before. As they approached, he noticed something a little more peculiar, he wasn't greeted by the horrendous odor, and they should have started to smell it by now. He got a dozen steps past, in a direction he hadn't been the day before from the stream, when he found footprints, bare tracks in the mud. Garrett turned to look back in the direction of the stream, Naomi still hanging back. He could see where he had picked up Growler clearly from there, and his heart raced, wondering if someone had been watching him the day before and again, he thought about the low rumbling growl.

When Naomi got there, she placed her foot next to the print. It was even smaller than her own. "You smell anything?" Garrett questioned.

Naomi took a moment to gather herself and look around. "Nothing."

"Yeah, me either. Yesterday here, it was ripe." He looked up and now all around him but saw nothing that caught his attention. The birds flowed through the tree line, starting in and out toward them, much the same way they had done to him the day before. Garrett found where the tracks turned away, heading back inward. They followed them a hundred feet further into the woods until they seemed to disappear.

"Garrett." He turned to his left to see his wife with her hand placed over her mouth.

He hadn't even noticed it until she said it, but the smell was there lingering in the air, the distinct funk they had both smelled the day before. He pulled the revolver and held a tight grip on the handle as he walked around the trees, trying to pick up the trail again.

"Watch your step," he said, circling around Naomi.

The smell was even stronger by her. He walked in circles around where they were, hoping to pick up tracks or find the source of the smell, but he never found either. He saw the old, rusted trap shining in the sunlight, but even from where he was standing, he could see blood shining in the sunlight on the trap. He approached it being more cautious than before, he had never seen one in person, but he knew exactly what it was when he saw the jaws clamped closed, a bear trap. He looked around it, making sure there were no others close by. He put his hand on the trap clearing the wetness, and it came back a dark red.

"Someone's been trapping bear here. Not even sure if that is legal these days," Garrett quickly said.

"It's certainly unethical," Naomi was standing not far from him now, looking around. "You think someone has snagged a bear?"

"How would a bear have gotten out of it, though? For that matter, how would anything have gotten out of it and gone very far?" Garrett questioned.

"Or maybe whoever set it came back, got it, and left a part of a carcass here, and that is what we're smelling," Naomi questioned.

"But the smell seems to move… as if whatever it is is wounded, and one of its limbs is decaying and rotting while still attached, if that's possible." Garrett ran a hand through his hair.

A limb cracked somewhere nearby, catching their attention and causing them to look up at the nearby trees. He slowly walked in the direction of the sound, with Naomi a few paces behind. He was careful, watching for more tracks and his 30/30 at the ready. They came to a clearing, and there he saw the tracks again. There was a couple of distinct set of traps now, one moving in the soft dirt, but couldn't actually tell how big the person who left the tracks were and the barefoot prints near an old oak tree. He followed the barefoot tracks for a while until he lost them underneath an old oak tree.

"Go that way." Garrett motioned to his left. "But please be very careful and watch your step."

"I will." He watched his wife circle out away from him as he put the 30/30 back around his chest, where it would be held in place without needing any aid. He took a long deep breath before he started off to the right of the large oak tree. He went about twenty feet, finding nothing, but increasingly he noticed the lack of the smell the further he got away from where they had found the trap. Maybe there was something there hidden away in the underbrush that he just wasn't seeing.

"Garrett!" he heard Naomi yell out. He didn't rush to her, still too worried about coming across another trap until he reached her.

"I think…"

Garrett could see the horror in his wife's expression. It was something he had never seen before as she bit down on her lip and looked away just enough to compose herself. "I don't think it was some animal that got caught in that trap, but someone." She took a long stick she had retrieved sometime since they separated, and she pointed at a set of tracks in front of her, the barefoot tracks, but this time, there was evidence of blood in the track. "What the hell is going on here, Garrett?"

He could hear the fear in her voice. His wife was a compassionate person, and he knew it would kill her to think there was someone out there on their property who was mortally hurt, and it went unsaid; with the small size of the tracks, it was either a young woman or a child.

"Not supposed to be anyone here." Garrett was angry. "We need to find whoever is out there." He looked around for a moment. "Hello!" he yelled. "Yell back if you can hear us… or something." He whispered the last part. "What if there are more of those God damn traps out here? One of those things would kill…" He couldn't help but think about how he had lost Growler the day before.

"There's a hiking trail that is in the national forest just outside of our property," she said. "The hiker could have come from there and got lost."

"Yeah, but who set the trap? Maybe it's been here since before we started to buy the property," he replied. "So, we need to make sure there are no others on our land and need to report it to the local game service." Garrett stepped out around her. "Hello!" he yelled out, "Are you out there?" We know you're hurt. We just want to help."

"Do you really think there are more traps out there?" Naomi questioned.

"It's a possibility," Garrett said, "and I don't want one of us getting caught in one. Damn thing looked like it was a hundred years old."

"And we need to find whoever got caught in it," Garrett positioned himself to look back in the direction they had come. "What I don't understand."

"Why aren't we finding tracks more often?" she said, acknowledging they were both thinking the same thing. "We're not finding any spot where they are dragging their leg, and whoever got caught in this trap is hurt."

"So, it doesn't make sense. Maybe they're not hurt as bad as we think they are," he said with a pause, turning back and looking at his wife. "They're wounded, and they haven't gone far, but they are out here somewhere."

"Hello!" she yelled out. "We're here to help. Let us know where you are." They both took a long pause to look at each other and listened to the wilderness, but nothing was making any sound. Birds again flew through the area, several between them not seeming to pay any attention, but at the same point, it was like they did it on purpose. "Is that the same type of birds that were acting strange with you yesterday?" she questioned.

He looked at her, and then in the direction where the birds had flown. "Yeah. The birds are acting unusual I don't know what it is." He ran his hand through his hair in frustration as he took a peek at his phone. "We've got maybe three hours before dark. Do you think you could go back and check on Growler, maybe call up Fish and Game and tell them what is going on here? I'm going to walk a little further around and see if there is anything else I can find."

"Okay, sure," she replied, obviously not too keen on going back by herself.

Garrett stepped up to his wife, putting his hand on her hip and pulling her close. "Promise you'll be careful on the way back, don't get in too big of a hurry."

"I'm not sure you should be out here after dark either," she said.

"I'll be careful," he couldn't help but let his free hand grab at the sling attached to the rifle.

"Promise," she said.

"I promise, I love you," he said, tightening his grip on her backside for a hard squeeze, and he got an immediate reaction in the form of a blush and a smile. He loved that they had been married for ten years, and he could still make her blush. Of course, if he were honest, she made him blush far more often than he did her.

"I love you," she responded before pulling away from him.

He waited till she was completely out of sight before he took a steadying deep breath and went about looking for more tracks. He was being extra cautious now about making sure he didn't run onto another trap. He sighed and kept looking and traveled quite a bit further into the woods until he saw an old brush pile and at once noticed the blood. He looked at a near deadfall. The top of the tree made a large enough structure that something could have been hidden within. It was so dark within the brush that he couldn't see.

"Hello, is there anyone in there?" he questioned, sticking his hand in and pulling at the brush, trying to get a better look. It was then he saw something that looked like fabric sticking in the brittle limbs. He raced, plucking it from the branch. It was almost as thin as paper, and you could practically see through it, but it wasn't cloth. He held up the piece of material into the sunlight. It looked almost like a spider web hidden in the material in the light. It looked and felt like a texture of a butterfly wing to his touch and even left a little bit of residue where he pinched it, but it was so large there was no way it came from a butterfly. The butterfly would have almost been the size of a human child. He took a closer look at it, and he recognized it almost like tiny veins running through it, and then when he pinched it just a little bit harder, it almost felt like it was molded to his finger for a moment. Garrett dropped it into the air, and to his surprise, it floated down into his other hand as it waited.

"What the hell is this?" he muttered. He stuffed it into his shirt pocket and continued to investigate the brush. He crawled onto his knees, and inside the pocket hidden within the deadfall, there he found a whole bed of blood. He placed the tips of his fingers in the blood and looked at it. It was almost black to the touch and was old. He smelled it, but there wasn't any detectable order, and this was not what was leaving such a found smell all around the property. Garrett crawled his way back out of the deadfall and stood up tall, looking around. There was no way whoever was bleeding was far away from where he was standing now and had no doubt they could hear him.

"Hey, you out here! I want to help!" he yelled. Then the eerie feeling took hold. *What if they can't answer*?

Chapter Seven

Garrett

The entire way back to the camp, Garrett walked cautiously and with purpose. He had not planned on being in the woods after dark, but it came on before he had even known it. He had still been messing around with the deadfall when he noticed the shadows were growing more evident. He had his gun ready at every sound, and he knew that was a bad thing. This was how people got hurt. He was so stuck on trying to figure out what bled out in that deadfall. Its blood smelled almost sweet. The bear trap itself bothered him as much as anything. There was something odd about it. He would make his way back to it tomorrow morning at first light. He had to see it better for himself. He was grumbling with regret for leaving it to begin with. He could see the light from the fire in the distance. He was thankful his wife knew to make it once she got back to camp, even if it meant he would have to cut more firewood the next day.

Garrett heard something crack behind him. He turned to put the gun toward the darkness. "Hello? I've got a gun."

He pulled the hammer back on the gun, preparing to fire if needed. He knew a lot of people who always itched at the chance to shoot an intruder, or anyone for that matter. But that wasn't him. Guns were a tool. He listened, but all he could hear was his own heavy breathing in the darkness. He turned to look back toward the fire, always keeping his gun ready. When he got to the fire, he stopped, letting his hands warm, looking at the bruises on the back of his knuckles. The blood had dried up there now, and his wounds were past needing cleaning. He had spent so much time worrying about what was lurking on the property that he had forgotten to take care of his own hand, and it was sore. He needed a shower more than anything right now, though.

"Honey, you here?" he questioned out loud. He saw the camper shift just a little bit as she stepped up to the front door, "We were worried about you. We're getting ready to start some dinner. Did you find anything?"

"I found some more blood," he said before he looked back to the fire. "But nothing else.".

"Did you hear anything out here?" he questioned before looking back toward the darkness.

"Nothing. I did call Fish and Game and updated them on what happened, said they'd try a send someone by here tomorrow but didn't sound too sure if you ask me," Naomi replied, and he could see the disappointment on her face. "I did consider maybe the warden that was here the other night might be the one who left the bear trap. Maybe I'm just being paranoid."

Garrett hadn't thought about it directly, but now that his wife had put it into words… "Would explain why he was up in here before daylight the other day. And I'm willing to bet he knows the terrain. I hate to think about that right now."

Garrett remembered the fabric in his pocket. He pulled it while walking to the RV and stepped inside behind her before setting it on the counter. "You ever see anything like this?" he questioned, taking a leaning position on the counter. He watched as his wife inspected the material and held it up to the light.

"It's beautiful. What do you think this is?" she questioned.

"I don't know. I found it on the old deadfall branch back where I found all the blood," Garrett said. They both looked at each other with confusion. "How's Growler doing?" he looked to the puppy sitting back in the corner of the trailer. The dog was huddled with his back to the wall, trying to meld into the shadows.

"His foot is sore. I cleaned it again and rebandaged it, he cut it pretty deep, but I think he is going to be okay," Naomi replied. "How is your hand?"

"I'll live," Garrett said as he looked at his busted-up knuckles.

Naomi stepped to the sink, grabbing a bottle of antiseptic and a rag. He wanted to pull his hand away as she got closer, but she held hers out for him to put it in almost like she would have to do a child.

"In the morning, I'm going head on back and get that trap and get it off our land. But mostly, I want to travel a little further toward the edge of the property and see if I can see any fresh sign," he replied as he winced at her cleaning the wound on his hand.

"I tried to lift it when I came back by it, but I couldn't do anything with it. I left it right where we first found it. The thing is distorted with age, but there was something… I don't know. When I touched it, it was like it had an electrical charge to it. Does that make sense?" Naomi was taking her time to make sure all of his hand was clean.

"No, not really," he said, "but right now, nothing's really making a whole lot of sense. So, I'm going to take both field cameras you picked up to see if we can catch what all is going on out there. And we still need to find whatever got caught in that trap, and if it is suffering, it needs to be put out of its misery."

"Not to change the subject or anything, but what are we going to do about the old house?" Naomi questioned.

"I don't know," he replied, "that could be useful. Maybe even the house can be renovated, but now, we need to worry about what kind of predators or—even humans—may be roaming around on this land."

"I agree, maybe I'll run into town in the morning to get a couple of extra cameras, and I may go talk to a game warden to make sure they know what is going on here," she said.

"Be careful. You may be on to something about the game warden that was out here the other morning," he replied. "I guess looking for more traps and people when everything else." There was a long pause between the two of them. "So, what are you making for dinner."

"Some cooked chicken with squirrel gravy," she said with a large toothy grin.

Garrett placed his hand on her hip, pulling her in close and giving her a kiss. Naomi wrapped her arms around Garrett's neck. "You're not serious about the squirrel gravy, are you?"

"No," Naomi said as she wrinkled her nose.

#

Garrett was up an hour before daylight. He half expected to hear something smacking the trees nearby the moment he stoked up the fire, but there was nothing. He strapped the pistol to his side and had a backpack, complete with a couple of field cameras. He was only waiting for daylight now. Growler hung at his side by the fire. Seeing him out of the RV for more than just a bathroom trip was good. The puppy sat at his feet, being more attentive and loving toward him than he had ever been.

"I hate to cut this short, little guy." He plucked Growler from the ground and held him tightly, approaching the RV. It would be daylight soon. He carefully closed the door before starting off from the camp. He was less than a hundred feet from the warmth of the fire when the sun started to break over the horizon.

He made double time getting back to where they had found the bear trap, with a handheld axe attached at his hip and pistol on the other, plus the backpack. He found the exact location where the trap had been, but it was gone. He found something he was hoping not to find, a large track in the soft mud. He set his own foot beside the large print, and his heart started to race. It was more than double in size than his own, both in length and width. He looked around where he found it and quickly found more of the same abnormally large tracks heading in the direction he had the day before, in the direction where he had found the blood in the deadfall. He kept walking until he could see the deadfall in the distance. What bothered him the most was that the smell was gone just like the past few days, and so were the tracks.

Garrett walked until he got to the deadfall, pulling the small axe from his side, and started clearing out some of the small, easy-to-cut limbs of the deadfall. When he got to where he had cleared enough of the limbs that he wouldn't have to crawl inside, he put the axe away and stepped inside. "What happened here? What the hell is going on around here?" he questioned mostly to himself now, with his mind firmly stuck on the abnormally large tracks he found.

Snap.

Garrett turned to look back in the direction of the sound pulling his pistol in a swift motion, but there was nothing. At least there was nothing he could see. He set the camera on a small limb on the inside of the deadfall, pointing out, half wondering if there was something else watching this same place and would pay it a visit once he was gone.

He made it about a hundred feet from the deadfall when he started smelling smoke, and more than anything, he was too far away from camp for it to be from the fire. But there was more than just the smell of smoke, the distinct smell of meat having been fried. He kept going till he found a clearing probably ten feet in diameter. Garrett lowered to put his hand over the ashes and could still feel the heat coming from them. He grumbled. Garrett stood, looking around at the ground. It had been a cold and foggy night, leaving a dew on the ground around where the fire had been built. Garrett ran his hand through his hair in frustration, taking in his surroundings. There was nothing nearby watching him, but he felt an eerie chill. He circled the fire until he found more tracks. There were a distinctive set of new tracks here, dog tracks. Much like the other tracks, these were abnormally large, and he imagined they were even larger than the average timber wolves. It made his heart skip a beat. He stood, looking around. He wanted to yell out, tell people get the off his property, but the words got caught in his throat, and he let out an audible growl of disappointment The last thing he really wanted to do as he lowered himself to get a better look at the new intruders prints.

#

Naomi

There wasn't an antique shop in Elkhorn City. She had found a couple of small shops she visited that said they were antique shops on the outside, but once she was inside, she quickly realized that they were nothing more than small yard sale-style stores with items that could have been bought at most big box stores. Naomi found her way to the oldest pawn shop slash hardware store around; it even had an established in 1944 just outside the main door. She had been here the day before and remembered once she had escaped it the first time, telling herself she wouldn't come back. But now she stood just outside the door looking in as she took a deep breath, the last deep breath of fresh air, before she opened the screeching old metal door and entered.

The isles in the store were too narrow for buggies, let alone for two people to pass as they walked through. The floors were scuffed and dirty, and half the florescent lights in the store were flickering with their frustration casting shadows all around the already spooky store, and a few were not even working, adding to the atmosphere. The worst part she didn't want to revisit was the smell of cats, though she hadn't seen any the day before she knew somewhere nearby were a lot of cats who weren't being well kept care of and it left a funk seeping from the walls of the old store.

"Can I help you, Miss?" she turned, having not seen the man behind the counter when she entered the store.

"Hey," she said, walking up to the counter. "How are you? I bought a couple of game cameras in here yesterday, was wondering if maybe you had any more?"

"I'm fine young lady, how are you?" an older man, mostly bold and dressed in a too-small flannel, said. He was wearing a towel around his neck, sitting behind the counter with a rolled-up newspaper in hand as if he was using it to swat at flies. She hadn't noticed any hanging around the counter. He wasn't the person who had waited on her the day before. He was a much older and heavier version of the young man who had sold her the previous cameras.

"I will have to look in the back," the man replied with a grunt as he slid down off his chair, the old metal frame making almost as much noise as he did in the movement. He walked into the back. The man had a strange, almost perplexed look on his face before he disappeared behind the curtain.

A woman in an automatic wheelchair rolled out into the room and up to her. "How are you, young lady?" Her voice was cracked and had a since of wisdom to it that only came with age, though sometimes she wondered if that was true or if it was just age that made a person sound that way. Something that had been verbally beaten into her mind when she was young about getting wiser and smarter as one got older. She was easily eighty to eighty-five, perhaps, but she had a look on her face of amusement and curiosity. The woman rolled up to her so close Naomi had to take a step back so she wouldn't roll over her toes.

The wind swished around her and the moment passed Naomi she wanted to gag. She coughed trying not to be rude as she ran her hand across her mouth and nose, the smell of cleaning spray and cat pee. "I'm sorry," Naomi said trying to cover her mouth. "I've got a bit of a cold."

"My son tells you were the woman who bought the cameras yesterday. You new to town?" She pulled up next to the counter with her eyebrows raised in a way to say she wasn't welcome.. Her hand trembled as she held her palm upright as if to shake Naomi's. Her skin was leathery and wrinkled. She did just as the old woman wanted, and her grasp was surprisingly strong but cold to the touch sending a chill up Naomi's arm.

"My husband and I just bought a house maybe twenty minutes from here," Naomi replied, finally rescuing her hand from the older woman's grasp.

"So, you are the ones who bought the old Johnson's place." The old woman's facial features twitched almost in anger as she looked from Naomi back to her son who had moved back to his spot behind the counter.

"I think that is who the realtor said owned it before," she replied.

"Ought not done that," the old woman said, and Naomi imagined if she'd had teeth, she been clinching her jaw in anger. "Ought not done that without consulting some of the locals, anyways. That old house has a curse upon it. Maybe you won't believe those sorts of things not being locals and all, but I believe it's just a whole lot of unfortunate incidents."

Naomi felt her face flush with an anger of her own, "We are locals, born and raised not far from here just moved back to get closer to home to retire," Naomi regretted speaking up the moment she had.

"If you've moved away from here, you're no longer a local," the old woman said as she leaned forward almost aggressively in her chair. The wisdom seemed to go out of the older woman's voice, replaced with disdain and vile. Though she imagined it wasn't addressed just to her but to everyone this woman came in contact with.

"A curse?" Naomi questioned. She looked to the son behind the counter and got an almost apologetic smile from him before she turned back to the angry old lady in the chair.

"Well, Johnson died four years ago." She looked to her son, who just sat right back down at his place behind the counter. "Yeah, four years ago Johnson died. He wasn't what you call the friendliest of people. Well, that's not necessarily true. He was friendly when he was younger, but I knew him well before he went off his rocker. I think I graduated a couple of years after him in school." She again looked to her son and then the stones in her hand. "He was friendly enough back then, though a little on the odd side. But I don't know, I don't really recall when he turned into some crazy recluse. I'm sure it was before he killed that boy."

"He killed someone?" Naomi questioned, starting to wonder if maybe the old Mister Johnson had left the beartrap way back in those hills.

"Yeah, there wasn't much outrage over it, really. The boy was trespassing, after all. Half the population around here likes to boast about trespassers being shot. Well, old Mister Johnson did it… never served a day for what happened. I don't think the old sheriff back then even questioned the reasons why, but there were mumblings that the boys went there for other reasons." The old woman again looked at her son.

"There were other incidents?" Naomi questioned.

"Besides the shooting?" she questioned. "Well, Johnson's great granddad was killed by a couple of dogs, apparently, and his grandmother committed suicide by hanging, not exactly the womanly way to go, but who am I to argue with how someone chose to spend their eternity in hellfire?" Naomi gritted her teeth as the old woman's face reddened even more as she looked down at her twisted, broken legs in front of her. "Johnson's dad, I'm not sure, cancer maybe… I think the parents before that died in a freak flood up in that holler behind the old house." Naomi thought about the deep hole of water at the waterfall she had found. "But that's what they say. I don't know how much truth there is to any of that. And then there were others before, dating all the way back to the 1800s, people dying on that land for some unforeseen reasons. You may go by the library, and they could help you with some old newspapers if they still have them." For a moment, Naomi thought about the supposed Bigfoot sightings, even by her own husband. "Johnson himself used to be a church goer, never missed a service… never known him being married or having so much as a scandalous relationship worth gossiping about… and trust me, in this town, we would have known, it would have been all of the Sunday morning conversations if he had. But one day at church, he showed up with that girl. You remember her, don't you, Son?"

The son just scoffed, trying to ignore her question, but Naomi caught a little something else in the man's glance, he was keeping something to himself, and he looked at Naomi with a slightly upturned eye.

"Anyways, he showed up one day with his granddaughter, he called her. I guess she was maybe twenty… but that was the last time either of them ever came to church. I remember she was dressed in oversized clothes, and her hair was white as snow, but she was young, and all the boys were fascinated with her. You were one of them, weren't you, son?" The woman scoffed as she picked up the fly swat and slapped it to the counter at a fly Naomi hadn't seen. "Even though they couldn't tell anything about that girl with her baggy clothes. I don't understand why everyone was so up in arms about her."

"The preacher that day called her a demon. She had these almost purple eyes and snow-white hair, the preacher got up front of everyone and started preaching about the evils of women and makeup, obsession and lust, and almost all of it was directed at her. It wasn't her fault that all the boys were so dumbstruck by her. She was goddamn beautiful… even now I think about her." the man gritted his teeth, trying to look anywhere but at his mother. His mother again swatted at a fly and the man's face turned redder.

"Yeah, well, that was the last time he ever brought her into town. In fact, the last time he ever came to church. It was that week he killed that boy, and the gossip was the boy had gone by to see the granddaughter," the old woman said. "Now, this old woman needs her beauty sleep. But if I were you, I wouldn't stick around very long. I'd sell out and leave."

"I appreciate your help," Naomi said with a pause, before she could even complete her task, the old woman was gone into the back.

Naomi was walking outside when the man called out to her. "They say Johnson was crazy, but he wasn't crazy. Some used to drive by his place just hoping to get a glance at her on the grounds, even after he killed that boy. That boy he killed was a friend of mine, he told me he saw her a couple of times there when he'd go sneak onto the old mans land. I told he shouldn't have done that but he didn't listen to me or anyone who tried to talk sense into him. I don't know how much of it is true, but he said she ran around the property naked. I hate to admit it that made me want to go there even more. But there was a little something about that girl that just drove all of us mad, really. And he hardly came to town, once a month to get his grocery and supplies, and never saw her again."

"Let me ask you this—you know anybody still using bear traps in this area?" she questioned.

"Bear traps?" he questioned. "No, those things are inhumane. I don't know anyone around here would use anything so barbaric."

"Yeah, that's my thought," she replied.

"Mister Johnson always packed around a journal and pens. If you get into that old house, there is a good chance you'll find some of them, and maybe if you do, find his granddaughter. Tell her we're all sorry for how we treated her. Just be careful." The man turned and started back to the store. Naomi didn't move until he disappeared. Naomi gathered herself and took a long deep breath of fresh air.

<u>*Chapter Eight*</u>

Garrett

Sweat beaded on Garrett's forehead as he stared blankly at the large dog imprints in front of him. It wasn't until an angry mosquito buzzed in front of his eye and he attempted to swat it did it bring him back to reality. "Shit," he mumbled to himself looking up at the sky. He imagined something big enough to leave the weighted track in front of him should stand out. Garrett stood running his hand through his shaggy hair and spat in the direction of the monstrous track giving it a look before surveying his surroundings again. "Where are you?" he mumbled mostly to himself through gritted teeth.

The phone in his pocket buzzed stopping him from looking for anyone or anything that may be watching him back. He snapped a photo of the tracks enlarging it to get a better view. He gathered himself taking a deep breath before heading in the direction of the back of the property.

He found a couple more deadfalls, all the same as the first one, each had a distinct hollowed-out feel to the inside. The fourth one had limbs broken and almost like they had been chewed through to create the void. There were leaves on the inside as well as straw forming a makes shift bed. This left him puzzled. Something had been sleeping in these deadfalls, and it obviously wasn't the hunter with the dog. Something smaller that could slip inside and hide when it needed.

As he came out of the last deadfall, the birds were all sitting around him, all watching him. He caught at least twenty sets of eyes glued on him, the same birds swooping in and out of the woods the past few days. He stood, taking a moment to look at all of them he could see, almost afraid to step forward too fast, feeling as if they might attack. There was something recognizable in those eyes staring at him, a consciousness and understanding of what they were looking at, but this left him feeling more on edge and uncomfortable. Again, a snap in the distance of a tree line broke his concentration as he pulled a pistol looking on that way.

"Damn it," he said out loud, and he was jumping at shadows, but the eerie feeling was there. Something had been following him not just today, but the entire time he'd been on the property. It was still several hours before dark, but he decided then it was time to head back. He set up the remaining field cameras all in the general facility of the camp. He checked his phone to make sure they came through properly and that any pictures they took he would get almost instantaneously.

He returned to the camp. He checked the RV, and there was no sign of Naomi or her truck. She still wasn't back. Garrett decided then he needed to cut some more firewood as he took to the saw and a nearby stack of trees he'd lined up for cutting.

#

Naomi

Naomi hesitated the moment she pulled off of the old road stopping just near the old concrete block structure that implied the start of the driveway up to the old house. "What are you doing," she mumbled to herself as she pulled in front of the house, the ruts where she pulled in mostly deteriorating because of water run off somewhere around the unkept yard. The moment she got out of the truck, she felt as if she had stepped into a horror movie, and a chill ran up her back, feeling as if something was watching her. She took a moment to gather all her courage as she dug at the keychain the realtor had given her, there were only a couple of keys on it, and she assumed both went to the house. She carefully approached the old dwelling watching all the windows facing the road. It was still on her mind just how much Growler disliked the looked of it. She expected any moment to see the curtains move or some figure standing watching her as she approached but neither happened.

The house was old two-story, and as she approached the front porch, she could see access to a cellar where she imaged old canned food and storage had been kept, and most of all, she could see the old, rusted padlock. Paint on the wood siding was way past needing to be scraped and redone, and she had seen several rotted spots on the edges of the porch as she approached the steps, the bottom of which was completely rotted through. Naomi again glanced at the old cellar doors and the rusted lock, detouring and picking up the lock on its rusted chains. She placed the smallest of the two keys inside, and it popped open, much to her surprise with how rusted it appeared. She pulled the chains through the rings and let if fall to the ground, then took the one handle and pulled the door open. She turned the light on her phone on and looked at the wooden steps leading into the musty basement, the smell was enough to cause her to cover her mouth, and she quickly took a step back. She quickly decided to leave the door open in hopes of allowing the moldy smell to escape as she returned to the porch.

Naomi stepped up on the old Victorian-style porch, and with each step she took, the wood underneath her feet creaked and cried. She slowly placed the remaining key in the old deadbolt but found it was already unlocked. It slowly crept open into the darkness. She stepped inside and instantly noticed the hole in the floor to her right. She could see animal droppings all around the floor and a makeshift nest in a corner. She figured at least a raccoon or opossum had taken residence here since Mister Johnson's passing. She stepped through the house, being careful of every step she took, making sure she wouldn't fall through the structure. She entered the kitchen, looking around. There were a lot of boxes everywhere sitting on stuff, turned over. She imagined the intruder had also taken to investigating the boxes to make sure there were no scraps left behind. There were cobwebs and spider webs clinging everywhere. She took a nearby old broom handle and knocked the one hanging in the door down, hoping whatever hideous spider wasn't still around watching. She decided then she would keep the broom handy just in case she came across any other complex silk structures that might try to lash out at her. She took a moment to inspect the boxes herself, and a lot of old canning jars seemed to fill most of them.

Naomi stepped into the mud room beyond the kitchen, there wasn't much in this room but the door leading to the outside. She could see the road heading up the road to where the RV was parked. She turned through a door just outside the mud room and entered a long hallway. She opened the nearby door leading to a nearly empty bedroom. There were some cargo boxes she would have to inspect later. She found a bathroom next to it. A smell seemed to engulf her the moment she let it open, much like the smell coming from the cellar. It didn't take much imagination to figure out why the two smelled so foul and comparable. She quickly shut the door and went to another nearby door, another bedroom just as empty as the last except for the ceiling, which looked completely engulfed with dust and spiderwebs.

Last was a living room area. There was an old couch that was nearly broken in two, an old-style television, and a VHS player, complete with several old tapes sitting on top. She checked them out and instantly recognized them as older westerns. Apparently, Johnson wasn't a materialistic guy or hadn't moved into the modern era. She thought there was also the possibility that rogues might have come in shortly after his passing and taken anything of value.

There was nothing extraordinary here to look at. It was all old, not even antique old, just makeshift and simple, not that she thought anything was wrong with that. She ran a hand through her hair, feeling the web between her fingers. She hadn't even realized she had walked through any. She violently shook her hand, trying to get it off, but mostly she wanted to ensure no spiders were left behind. She was beginning to wish she had put the ballcap on for no reason other than to protect her head from unwanted visitors.

Naomi turned back to the stairway just inside the front door, careful not to get too close to the nest. The stairs creaked with almost every step she took upward, but she didn't stop until she reached the top. She could only see three doors in the large hallway. She went to the back of the hallways, first coming onto a chair sitting in front of the window, the window looked out up the road, and she thought she could see smoke from their fire from the chair. She took a seat in the old-style kitchen chair, and it was the first thing there that seemed not to have aged. It didn't scream at her when she sat.

The first room she came to was some sort of sewing room, complete with an old sewing machine and several old blankets and materials. An old solid oak teacher's desk was sitting on one side of the room. She went to this desk and at once opened the drawers that would open, but she only found the one locked. She found a small crowbar in the top drawer, shoved it into the top of the locked drawer, and pried it open. At first, she didn't think it would open, but after a little more pressure, it broke free. When it opened, there were several journals on the top. She opened the first to see handwritten logs in the journal, and she remembered what the guy at the pawn shop had said. It was handwritten. She gathered them all on top of the desk, found a nearby old grocery bag, and put them in it so she could take them back to camp. As she stepped out into the hallway, she set the bag near the top of the stairs and wanted to inspect the last two rooms.

The first one was a bedroom of some sort. There was a king-sized bed in the room. It was dusty and old, just like everything else in the house. The final room was a small room. She instantly knew the difference in this room compared to all the rest of the house. It was clean. It had been cleaned recently. As if someone had been living there for the past few days. A small bed was pushed up in the corner with fresh sheets, and other things scattered about the side of the room. This room had been lived in since the death of the earlier owner, and this caused her heart to race as she turned and looked back at the open door. She took note of everything in the room before she left. She rushed back to her vehicle, quickly making her way back to the camp.

Naomi got back to the camp and quickly spread all the notebooks out on the table. She spread them out, looking for what would probably be the oldest. The date on the first page was 1944. There was a drawing of fairy wings all over the page and one small journal entry.

November 30th, 1944

This is crazy. I think I'm loosing my mind. I have no other way of putting it, and if I'm being honest, I think Richard might have given me something at school today in my drink. I have no other way to explain what it was. I feel like I need to start with this, I don't journal, but I feel like I need to get this down on the page so I don't burst. I saw something today that I can't quite explain, and every time I try to wrap my head around it, I think I'm crazy.

The cows were missing when I got home from school, and Dad believes it may snow tonight. Any other time he wouldn't have worried about them; they are always here in the mornings when I get up for school. Dad thought I was old enough to go on my own. Like so often before, I begged just to go on my own, so you can imagine my surprise when he agreed. He just wanted me to take my.22 and maybe bring a couple of squirrels home if I had the chance, but he stressed how much he wanted me to be careful.

I got my rifle, and I headed to the back of our property. So often when they don't come home, that is where they are, the old waterfall. Everything went smoothly. Maybe it's because I didn't have to wait around for Dad. He's starting to slow with his age. Might be part of the reason he let me go on my own this time. His hips are starting to bother him. I even got a couple of squirrels for dinner before I got to the waterfall.

I crept up to where I could see the waterfall, sometimes we'll see deer there, and I didn't want to spook them. That is when I saw her. She was waist-deep in the water. Her wings, I just couldn't take my eyes off her, this bright purple silk-like material. The cows were there drinking from the water where she bathed. A couple of deer and more crows than I think I have ever seen in one spot my whole life. It was like one of those drawings from the magazine Richard sometimes brings to school with him. I just couldn't believe what I saw.

I rushed home, leaving the cows behind. I wanted to tell Dad. Not for one moment did I ever doubt what it was I saw, and when I told him, he just gave me a look. He questioned if I had been in his moonshine. He told me not to tell Mom...

I truly think I saw an angel.

The next page was a picture of a fairy leaning over a waterway, and it was obvious the fairy was crying. The next page had been written in big, bold letters, though it wasn't an actual journal entry.

Are fairies real? It was very real. I think I saw a fairy.

The next page was a drawing of a wing, and Naomi couldn't help but notice the similarities to the wing Garrett had found the day before. She gave it a glance, still sitting on the countertop. The drawing was picture quality. Johnson was very talented. The wing looked identical. She flipped over to the next page to another drawing of a woman with fairy wings. She was very well-built and voluptuous, with big breasts, hips, and a big smile. Most of all, those four big wings attached to her back, the size she would imagine an angel, and the shape of butterfly wings. They were tall and glorious and engulfed the entire page the way he had drawn them. Naomi took a moment to admire the drawing before flipping to the journal entry on the next page.

March 1st, 1945

It's been a rough few months. At least every other day, I've gone back to the waterfall, and I've yet to see her again. Dad joked about getting me put in an asylum.

I saw a footprint today, a barefoot print on the side of the water. And I had that feeling that something was watching me. So just as I was thinking I was going to lose my mind, I think I really did see her. I won't continue to look for her, I'm going to give her space, and maybe one day, I'll catch a glimpse of her again.

June 23rd, 1950

Over five years have passed, I went away to school, and I came back a couple of days ago to put my father to rest. He apparently was in pain for quite some time, and the doctor says he is better off now. I hate that he kept his illness from me and my mother. I took the horse out for the first time in years, and I saw her again, and she saw me before she flew away.

July 13th, 1950

Mom isn't well. I've been having to spend most of my free time with her when I'm not at work, but the coal mines are taking a lot out of me. I don't like working down those mountains. Feels like any moment, everything is going to collapse in around me. Mom told me a story about something Dad was keeping from me about the fairies. I can't believe he was keeping it from me; let me think I was going crazy… even joked that I was crazy, but he knew. I don't think Mom meant to tell me. She's not always in touch with herself. Doctor says she may have early-onset of dementia. I saw the fairy tonight at sunset when I only wanted to spend some time with myself. She was there standing with a young cow picking at blackberries on the bush… it was like something out of a painting.

July 14th, 1950

Something woke me in the middle of the night, like a dog howling. And I saw something else… not the fairy, it was standing in the middle of the road out in front of the house. I have never seen someone so big in my life… him and his dog.

The next page had a drawing of a large man, all dark, hanging in the shadows of the road with a large menacing dog standing at his side. She'd imagined it with the bulk and the size of how he looked standing there in the shadows and at his feet, leaving a very unsettling feeling coming across her was a bear trap. She couldn't help but stare at the bear trap. It looked so much like the ones she'd seen the day before, and it left her feeling so sick to her stomach as she looked out the window to see if her husband was nearby. She closed the notebook and stepped outside. She looked around at the camp, and she could hear a chainsaw off nearby. She took a deep breath as she walked off in his direction.

Chapter Nine

Garrett didn't hear her come into the clearing where he was cutting wood. His ears were still ringing from using the saw. Growler ran past him, nearly clipping his leg, catching his attention. He turned just in time to see Naomi pluck him off the ground and instantly put the wild-acting pup into a position to rub his belly. Growler wagged his nubby tail with happiness. Garrett could hear the animal's happy whining.

"He has to be getting too heavy for that," Garrett said as he brought the bottle of water to his lips and watched as both his wife and supposed pup gave him a disagreeable glare. "How was town?"

"Well, I learned a little bit about the guy who used to own the property," she replied, taking a moment to look around the wilderness. "Did you find that bear trap?"

"I found where it was," he replied, instantly noticing the disappointment on her face. "But it was gone this morning, but I found something else." He pulled out his phone opening his pictures, showing her the picture of the footprints in the mud and the dog tracks. He had taken a picture of his own foot next to the track and how much larger it was. "Someone was there last night and took the trap with them."

"Yeah, well, I stopped by the old house on my way in, and I did a little bit of exploring. I found some journals that I think you ought to see," she said. His wife was pale after seeing the pictures, as if they were also expected to her. He gave her a curious look, watching as she put Growler back down. "I'm going to take him back to camp. Will you be along soon?"

"As soon as I get everything up," he replied, giving a glance at his tools. He watched as she and Growler walked away, and when they seemingly were out of sight, he started gathering his tools up.

He walked back to the camp overly cautious. Kept thinking about the oversized paw print every time he heard something in the woods, but it was a ground squirrel scurrying away. He couldn't help but wonder what was watching him. Even stopping and turning to investigate the growing darkness of the shadows, wondering if there was some large man standing there watching

When he reached the camp, his wife was feeding the horses, and Growler was running back and forth between her and the door as if the little dog had wanted her to go into the RV. Garrett was starting to think much the same about when it was dark out, how they should be spending less time outside when they couldn't see what was out there watching them. There was a sense of urgency in the dog that he had noticed before; he was growling and huffing as it ran. When Garrett reached the door, Growler leaped up onto him. Showing him some affection that he had never received from the animal before. He scratched it behind the ear and shifted his weight to lean into Garrett's shoulder as if to hug him. The dog was afraid of something. He trembled in fear.

"I know what you mean, buddy," the man said, turning back to look at his wife as she approached. They stepped into the RV setting the pup down on the makeshift couch just inside the door. He turned and slid in at the table with Growler and waited for Naomi.

He began to look through the notebooks and instantly stopped on the page of the drawing of the extremely large man. He huffed, mostly focusing in on the just as enormous dog at his side and the bear trap, and he realized why his wife seemed so out of it after he showed her the picture. "This is crazy, right?" He looked at his wife and then back to the drawing.

Then he flipped over a few dozen pages and stopped on the drawing of a woman's face. The beautiful large butterfly wings engulfed the entirety of the page behind her face. "So, what are you thinking?" Garrett said, looking at the drawing and then at his wife.

"Honestly, I don't know," Naomi replied.

"We can't be seriously thinking we've got fairies on our land. This is crazy, or that they even exist," he said, watching as his wife rolled her hand out and let the fairy tears fall on the table in front of them.

"Is it crazy? I mean, really," she said as she flipped the journal open until it was back on the page of the large man and pointed straight at the bear trap. "I don't know anymore."

Garrett laughed, but not a laugh of trying to push off what she was saying. He then focused on the drawing even more. He looked at the door and then back to his wife. "I've got the cameras out there. Maybe they'll pick up something tonight. Besides, we need to fix something for dinner." Garrett found himself wanting to change the subject.

"I've got one," she said with a smile. She crossed to the refrigerator, opened and pulled out a bottle of wine. She quickly opened it and poured two glasses. She leaned over, kissing him.

He retreated from her lips to the wine glass, where he took a big sip. He turned to the puppy nestled at his side, almost hiding from the outside world, stretched out almost completely, and could hear the puppy breathing heavily.

"Why the change in attitude?" He watched as Growler looked up at him through upward-turned eyes. The puppy wanted a moment. "Yeah, I don't quite understand either," he replied as if he were conversing with Growler. He turned to see his wife who was working on a couple of burgers. When the food was prepared, he shut up the journals, pushed them to the side, and took his plate and a glass of wine toward the door. He went and sat beside the fire, watching the dancing flames when Naomi took a seat beside him. Growler didn't join them outside.

"Do you think fairies are real?" Garrett questioned between bites. "I mean, we're still trying to make sense of it all. The journals seem very real, and with everything we've seen the past few days…"

"I don't know either," Naomi replied.

"With the way the birds in the area were acting, the blood trail, the footprints, the blood in the deadfall. There is just so much that doesn't really add up, and then there is the newest set of tracks added with the large canine track." Garrett took another drink of wine. "Something had bled that much; we should have been able to find a body. And then there was the fabric, the wing black fiber that he'd found at that fall. The barefoot prints, the large prints," he found he was repeating himself now.

"Unless we are truly dealing with something supernatural," she said. "It's what we are both thinking."

They both seemed to stare at the fire forever before one of them spoke again. He turned and looked back at the door of the RV. The pup was still inside and was refusing to come out into the darkness. "I think Growler is on to something. We're just not seeing what it has. I don't know if I can explain it, really. I'm hoping the cameras pick something up tonight; maybe we'll have a clearer picture come morning." Garrett was pouring himself another glass. He knew he wasn't going to sleep much tonight.

<u>Chapter Ten</u>

November 2nd, 1950

I know I should get better at updating this journal, but honestly, I only ever feel like writing into it when I see her. We buried my mom yesterday. I'm heartbroken, and I'm sitting up by the fire. Not going lie, I was drunk.

A stray dog wandered onto the property; a little white-faced dog looking like it had black freckles on its face. He's been here since the day I took my mother to the hospital, I guess it's a sign. I've been calling it Freckles. It may be a year old. He is sweet, really, wags his tail at me, doesn't bark or anything but will not get close to me. He just lingers around and eats the food that I give him. But he does seem to appreciate it. I hate the idea that maybe someone turned him out. I hate that people do such things.

It was barking at the darkness last night, but he wouldn't leave my sight. When I went to sleep, I let him in, but I didn't force him to let me get close; I just let him run past me into the warmth of the house. After about an hour, he wouldn't stop barking, and I came to the door. For a moment, I thought I saw her standing out there by the fire. It was no more than just ash by then, but we went out to investigate. I didn't really feel like sleeping. I wasn't near drunk enough. So, I stocked the fire back up, and sure enough, she was there. Freckles hesitated to go to her, but after a few moments, he did. She never looked at me, just stood there warming her hands by the fire. At first, I thought I was just that drunk.

This is the closest I've ever gotten to her. The closest I've ever been able to see those wings, and they're beautiful. She is beautiful. She looks like she stepped out of some fantasy novel but more real. Maybe she is what an angel is supposed to look like., not these feathered wings that they talk about in fables or songs. But these beautiful butterfly-like wings. She never spoke, just sat there petting Freckles, and the dog showed its appreciation by exposing its belly to her. Then Freckles did something completely unexpected the moment the fairy left the firelight. He came and sat down beside me, letting me scratch him behind the ear, and never even flinched. I'm man enough to admit I bawled like a newborn baby thinking about the fairy, but most of all, I thought about how much I missed my mother.

May 5th, 1955

Five years without seeing her, and today, she was perched on my roof when I got home from work. Funnily enough, Freckles was on the roof with her. I'm so curious; I had left Freckles in the house when I left. I have become so attached to the dog, and I don't like the idea of him getting in the road or some other animal getting after him. Did he crawl out the window? Or did she fly up and get him to come out the window?

I have the sneaking feeling this isn't the first time she has come by to see him. This might also explain why Freckles has a habit of running off into the wilderness at night and not coming back till morning. It had been so long since that first night that it never dawned on me that maybe that was where he was going at night.

By the time I made it into the house and upstairs, she was gone. She obviously isn't afraid of letting me see her now. One thing I don't like is how easy it would be for anyone driving by the front of the property to see her there on the roof. I think I'll nail the window shut and force them to use the back porch for their visits.

October 10th, 1955

Freckles lets me know when she's around now. Without hesitation, he'll give a low rumbling growl and wags his tail like crazy when she's around. I didn't see her the first few days, but she was standing there when he ran off right to the edge of the dark tonight. He dropped to his stomach and rolled over, and she patted his belly and scratched his ears, and she just stayed there with him for an hour before disappearing back into the wilderness.

October 12th, 1955

We went back into the hills again today, got up early left before the sun even broke the horizon. I had my reasons. I wanted to see her. She is in my dreams every night, and I just wanted to see her again. We made it to the waterfall just as the sun was coming up. She was there in the stream washing, washing her hair waist-deep down in the water. Freckles ran into the water and joined her. I can tell she loves that dog.

I didn't try to approach her, I didn't want to encroach on her territory, but I did sit by the bank of the water and watch the two of them play in the stream. She's beautiful, I realize today I can't let anyone else know about her. There is probably a government agency somewhere who knows about them. She can't be the only one out there in the world. But here in Kentucky, I'm so afraid that they would think she is something else. She looked at me while she and Freckles played and gave me an honest appreciative smile.

This is a secret I have to take to my grave.

December 25th, 1955

It's Christmas morning. I noticed something this morning with Freckles at breakfast. Maybe he's been doing it for the past couple of weeks and realized it. He's also moving slower. I found a lump on his back, and it broke my heart. I think he knows he is dying. How could I not have noticed?

December 25th, 1955

She's on my back porch with Freckles as I write this. She was waiting there when we got back from the vet. I can see her tears as she slowly pets him. She knows what is happening to him, and it breaks my heart even more.

April 4th, 1970

First time I'd seen her in fifteen years. I feel my own age catching up with me now, but she spoke to me today, just a whisper from the back porch. I saw her go to Freckles' grave. Never been able to bring myself to get another dog since him, but I think tomorrow I'm going to go to the pound. I think she needs another dog as much as I do, we both miss him very much, and maybe that's why she's been away for as long as she has.

My age is catching up with me. The strange thing is, and I guess I shouldn't think of it as being strange, she has an edge today since the last time I saw her. She doesn't look like she has aged a day this entire time, but there is a fierceness to her I can't quite explain. She still has the snow-white hair and the same complexion. I can't quite explain why it is I think she looks so different. I wonder how old she is. I would guess she looks the same today as the first time I ever saw her all those years ago

After she visited his grave, she came back, I took up my spot on the porch swing, and she sat on the steps, never spoke, just sat there, her wings fluttering, and she looked out into the woods. She gave me a look, her eyes that strange violet color, and she smiled.

April 06, 1970

I picked up two dogs from the pound today, both male, both mixed. Not sure what kinds they are, but they were in the kennel together and already familiar with one another. And they seemed so happy to see me. They had this look in their eyes that reminded me of Freckles, so I knew they were the ones I was supposed to pick up.

Both of them the moment I let them run into the wilderness, I was so worried that they wouldn't come back. I second-guessed myself every moment they were gone. About thirty minutes after they had left, they slowly strolled back out of the woods and came to join me on the porch. Both took up a position beside me. One, the bigger, darker one, I've started to call Myrle, rested his head on my leg. The smaller one, George, kept wagging his tail at such a frantic pace that I thought he would fly right off the porch. It wasn't long before I saw her standing just in the tree line, and even at that distance, I could see her smile.

December 25th,2017

Quit writing in this journal for a reason, and now I wonder where I go from here. I'm dying. The doctor said I maybe a year to live, two if God sees fit. I cried, and I cursed, and all I could think about was her. I don't know what she'll do even though I realize she's older than me. I've almost treated her like a daughter these past ten years, even took her to church though I never went back after that day they preached about demons and worshipping other things. She cried the entire time after the service.

We've kept dogs around the house ever since I picked up Myrle and George. But I don't want her to get lost in the world. I feel like she is some wild animal. Now that she realizes that not all humans are bad, she will come across the wrong one. And they'll hurt her. I'm having so many issues with that. It's breaking my heart. I hope

someone finds her and helps her keep her connection with people. The world is changing, and it's getting smaller all around us. Especially for her.

#

Naomi shut the journal; tears filled her eyes. She had waited until Garrett had seemed to doze off before she went to finish her reading. She wasn't sure how much time had passed. It was all she could think about, she wanted to see how the relationship between the fairy and Mister Johnson grew over time, but it had become even more than she had expected. She knew this wasn't just some fictional take on the old man's writing. There was really a fairy out there somewhere in the woods and in trouble. She looked at the dog at her side. Growler had his chin set on her knee. And she wondered how much of the journal was all about dogs and how the fairy reacted to them. Had Growler seen the fairy in their time here? She scratched the dog behind the ears.

"You're a good boy," she said, "aren't you?"

The dog let out a small bark that sounded like he was half-asleep. Naomi walked to the door and peeked outside; Garrett was apparently still asleep, sitting by the fire. She wondered if the fairy was out there somewhere watching them right now as she looked out into the darkness. More than ever, she knew the wild theories she and her husband were coming up with were real!

Chapter Eleven

Garrett

It had been hours since his wife had gone to bed, and he was still sitting out keeping the fire warm, his phone on a mobile charger at his side. He kept waiting for it to buzz, even looking at it from time to time to see if it was still working. It was frustrating. He wasn't sleepy, but his bones felt the cooling night air, like a ton of bricks lying upon him. A scream broke him from his daydream. He quickly grabbed the pistol from the table and rushed to the RV. As he opened the door, Growler fell out and ran into the darkness. Garrett watched as the small dog disappeared, whimpering and whining with almost every step he took. His heart sank as he stepped into the RV. His wife's normal pale complexion looked ghostly as she pointed a pistol with a trembling hand toward the window on the opposite side of the structure where she pointed the wavering firearm.

"What is it?" he asked, placing a steady hand on her trembling arm. She looked at him, mouth wide, trying to speak, but nothing came out. Her pupils were dilated from terror. He glanced to the table, realizing she hadn't gone to sleep but instead was awake reading the journals.

"I saw a face," she replied, her eyes filled with tears. Whatever she had seen truly scared her. He didn't hesitate to exit the vehicle circling around the other side until he reached the window where she had seen the face, but there was no one. Garrett shined the flashlight into the darkness around him but still saw nothing. He went to the window where she had seen it, he could see where fingerprints the visitor had left on the cooling glass, and he could see visibly inside where he thought his wife had been sitting reading the journals.

Garrett turned to face the darkness again, shining the light all around, hoping to see anyone or anything, his gun at the ready.

"Hello?" he yelled. "Come out, please! We want to help you!"

His phone buzzed in his pocket violently, causing him to adjust in shock. It continued to buzz and buzz as he retrieved it. The game camera closest to them had picked up something

. He looked at the pictures. Something large and dark had run past, coming in their direction. Without hesitation, he circled back around to the front of the RV, opened the door, and grabbed the shotgun from the driver's seat. He stumbled, reaching for the box of shells, wrenching one into the chamber before he finished loading the reserve with as many as it would hold. He wished he held more. He was also beginning to wish he had bought slugs instead of birdshot. He approached the RV door.

"Here, Growler!" he yelled out, looking in the direction the small dog had run, all while trying to keep his eye in the direction of where the cameras were positioned.

"What did you see?" Garret questioned as he looked at his wife. He felt like a ball being bounced as he tried to look in three different directions at once.

"It looked like a girl," she quickly replied. His wife was startled. He could see she'd been panting and maybe even second-guessing what she'd seen. She was obviously on the edge of a panic attack. It had been a while since she'd had one, but the way she was breathing brought back the memory of the night she'd had a miscarriage.

"The camera closest to camp also picked something up." Garrett took a moment to point in the direction of where the camera sat, trying to give her a distraction. "Coming this way, it's something different. Whatever had been peaking in the window didn't have time to get out there to start back this direction," he quickly said as he stepped toward the fire looking at their surrondings with the shotgun ready. He dropped the half box of shells onto the ground. "Whatever it was, it was large." He handed over the phone to her. She glanced at it and then returned to the vehicle, where she grabbed her pistol and stepped out into the night beside him. Naomi's color was beginning to come back to her, and he could no longer hear her labored breathing.

He looked at her. She was looking back in the direction Growler had run, "I'm sure he's fine," he said.

"He'll be fine," she tried to reassure herself.

Snap.

Garrett raised the shotgun to his shoulder and took a step forward. He'd heard something somewhere out of sight. It was only the one twig, so low he could not truly gauge where it had come from. His heart was racing just as his phone went off again. His wife had it, and she gasped when it buzzed. He glanced back at her as she looked at the picture that had been received.

"It went back the other direction." She held out the phone, showing the pictures fleeing video of something large moving back the other way from them. He quickly walked, grabbed his phone, walked past her head, and back to the RV. He hooked it up to his laptop and blew up the video, but even then, he couldn't really tell what the large figure was as it ran past the camera both times. It was just massive in size.

"I will go find Growler," he said as he got up and started out the door.

He started in the direction Growler had run; it didn't take long before he found the little dog. He hovered under a small limb just like the hollowed-out deadfall he had found with whatever had bled out in the woods. He coaxed Growler out after a moment and picked him up, starting back toward the RV.

"It's okay, buddy." He scratched the dog behind its ear, and it lay against him as if it hugged him again. He set the shotgun just outside the door. As he stepped up the steps, his wife was sitting at the table with the image pulled up and frozen on the screen. She looked at the notepad of the large figure that the Johnson man had drawn.

"You see the similarities?" She looked back at him as he entered, setting Growler down.

"Yeah, I see the similarities," he answered. He didn't want to, but it was all there in front of him.

"What the hell have we gotten ourselves into?" she questioned.

"I don't know," he sat down, putting his hand on the window. If he looked hard enough, he could still see the handprint the intruder had left behind. The fingerprints were half the size of his own. "And you say this looked like a young woman?" He looked back to his wife, who was watching him.

"Yeah, it looked like a woman's face, a round face, gentle, almost sweet-like, but she was staring at me, and her eyes were hollow, wild-like. Maybe it was the lights playing a trick on me, but they were a very unusual color," Naomi said, and Garrett noticed as she bit down on her lower lip as if she wanted to add something else but didn't. The bad part was Garrett knew without her saying what she wanted to add. Just like the fairy girl in the drawings.

"Like someone had lost a lot of blood." He looked at her and then back to the window. "If she's awake and she's been bleeding, she needs help. Maybe she came here hoping we would help her?" he said, standing and walking back to the door. He glared back at the frozen picture on the laptop screen. "I've seen something like that before." It caught his wife's attention as she also looked back at the screen. "You know all those field cameras that say they've caught Bigfoot? What does that look like to you?"

"All the Bigfoot sightings that they say happen in this area," Naomi again looked back at him. "Maybe there is something more to it than just people being crazy."

"Or maybe we're going crazy and don't even realize it?" Garrett said.

"But we're both seeing it," Naomi answered him.

"I don't know." Garrett grabbed his phone and put it back in his pocket before he walked back to the fire.

He shifted his seat so it wasn't facing the fire but toward the darkness where the closest field camera was set up. He set the shotgun across his lap as he sat a little bit more comfortably. It was just a couple of moments till he felt the nuzzle of Growler pushing up under him.

"Hey boy, what are you doing out here?" Growler kicked at the dirt until he jumped into Garrett's lap and laid down under the shotgun. "It's going to be okay," he said out loud. Growler acknowledged what he had said with a lick of his wrist. Garrett began to scratch him behind the ear, and he nestled into a ball in his lap.

#

Naomi

Naomi woke up and glanced at the door. It was still open. She got out and walked to the door, grabbing the pistol on her way out. The fire was getting low as she stepped out, and she noticed her husband slumping over. She grabbed a blanket just inside the door and approached him. She was amazed either of them had fallen asleep. She took a deep breath; she was awake now and would likely be up the rest of the night. Growler looked up at her, but he was nestled into Garrett's lap under the shotgun, and she could instantly tell the dog had no intention of leaving him. Naomi smiled; she was happy to see the two of them were finally bonding. She covered both up before she walked over, grabbed several lumps of wood from the pile, and tossed them to the fire. She put the gun on the table near her husband and took a long deep breath. She was watching the darkness, wondering if there was anything watching them now. She looked at his phone, making sure he hadn't slept through any notifications. None were waiting. She tied her hair back into a ponytail as she walked back to the RV. She was going to look over the journals again, but more than anything, she wanted to look closer at the drawings of the fairy. She couldn't get over the similarities between the drawing and the woman she had seen in the window. She turned her way back to survey the scene outside before shutting the door behind her.

The door clicked behind her, and she instantly saw the figure sitting in the back of the RV, huddled in a corner.

"It's all right," she said loudly, trying to keep her voice calm and friendly, "I'm not going to hurt you." She looked at the floor in front of her, and there was a blood trail leading all the way back to where she was huddled. "I can help you with your wounds." Naomi reached slowly to grab a nearby blanket and held it out in front of her. "You can cover yourself up. You have to be freezing." She approached two more steps and heard a low rumbling growl from the figure in the corner. She plucked her phone from the counter, carefully turning on the flashlight shining in her direction. Naomi stepped forward again, and the girl, fast as lighting, grabbed the blanket and pulled it around her. She covered her face up with the blanket. "It's okay. You're going to be okay."

Naomi walked back to the door turning the light on in the back of the RV. She watched as the figure popped its head out the front of the cover, and Naomi instantly knew she was right. The woman she had seen and the one in the drawing were the same. She had long straight white hair as perfect as a newly fallen snow, just as the guy at the pawnshop had described her. She poked her eyes out, a deep violet color she'd never seen before, but she knew it was natural, and they were hypnotizing in their beauty. She continued lower, and her lips were thin and chapped.

"We're not going to hurt you." She tried to reassure the young woman. "Are you wounded?" She knew she was, but she wanted to draw the woman in and get her to show her where she was hurt, but mostly she was afraid of making her feel like she was cornered. The last thing Naomi wanted was for the creature to lash out. No matter how beautiful she thought she was, there was an underlying hint of unspoken danger about her. "We found blood out there in the woods." Naomi looked at the floor and pointed at the blood trail leading to her. "Is it your blood?"

She nodded her head yes.

"Can you tell me your name? I am Naomi," she replied.

The girl mumbled something that she couldn't quite understand. She then removed her arm from under the blanket and pointed toward the countertop. Naomi looked to the surface and saw the cloth-like material that her husband had found on the deadfall.

"Is that yours?" Naomi questioned with curiosity. It was then the blanket seemed to shimmer under the movement of something at her back. "You can have it back now," Naomi said. The woman smiled slightly. "Are you hungry?" Naomi questioned. The girl shook her head yes. It was obvious to Naomi that the girl understood every word she was saying. "I've got sandwiches and chips." The woman smiled, exposing her teeth, and Naomi tried to hide the shock of seeing the large canines on the woman. They were natural predator teeth, and her heart raced, knowing she needed to be even more careful around her. Naomi stepped up to the refrigerator and opened the door, quickly pulling out lunch meat, bread, and a small bag of chips. She placed the chips on the table and started to make a plain sandwich. "Do you know what you like on your sandwich?" Naomi questioned, looking back at the young woman.

The woman gave her a smile. "Mustard."

"So you do speak," Naomi said, though she wasn't sure if the woman had even been speaking English the first time she'd spoken. Naomi reached the yellow bottle of mustard out, placing it on the table before the girl. Naomi smiled when she took the bottle and squirted a healthy amount of the yellow stuff on the sandwich before closing the bread back onto the meat. Naomi took a step back as the girl pushed the blanket off her naked body. Naomi was in shock. She hadn't even realized she was naked before, but now all she could do was stare in awe with her jaw open at the large butterfly-like translucent wings on the back of the woman. She couldn't take her eyes off them and could see where one had been torn. It was the same as the purple fabric sitting near her hand on the counter. The woman sat at the table and began to eat the sandwich and the chips so fast that she could only be half chewing her food.

"Slow down," Naomi said, and the woman looked up at her through her long eyelashes. "There is plenty. I'll make you another if you want it." The woman shook her head feverishly, apparent she would want another already. She saw the mustard on the girl's lower plump lip. Naomi didn't say anything as she quickly prepared the girl another sandwich. She'd turned and placed a napkin on the table next to the second sandwich just as she had finished off the first.

"Do you have a name?" Naomi questioned. The girl shook her head yes but wasn't speaking as she attacked the second sandwich. Naomi watched partially in shock, the rest in amazement as she finished off the second sandwich. "Do you want another?" The girl smiled as she finished stuffing a bite into her mouth. As Naomi watched her, she even thought she was gaining some color in her cheeks as she ate.

Naomi made the girl another sandwich. This time when she went to put the mustard on it, the girl grabbed the bottle and squirted more on the sandwich than either of the last two had on it combined, then started to eat it just as fast as the last one. "You're a fairy, aren't you?" Naomi questioned, watching her eat. The girl wasn't paying much attention to her now. Naomi shifted in her position, and as she did, the fairy scooted away from her in the booth. "No, no, no… I'm sorry…" Naomi held her hands out. "I'm going to get you something to drink. Water, maybe?"

The girl looked at her and twisted her head to one side. "Pop?"

Naomi smiled when she said it, shifted to get a pop from the fridge and set it in front of her. Naomi even popped the top open for her, and the girl seemed to light up as she took a drink. She imagined if pop was something the fairy loved, it had been an awfully long time since she had one. It wasn't like she could just drop in at a gas station and get her one, and that made her drop her head. The girl was wounded now, but she could see she was also lonely, and there had been so much she had missed out on with Mister Johnson gone.

The girl crushed the can in her hand and looked at her with almost childlike glee. "Another?"

"Yes, of course," Naomi said, retrieving another from the fridge. She didn't open it this time, watching instead as the fairy took a long fingernail and popped it open. Naomi couldn't help but glare at the sharp nails. They looked strong, strong enough to rip flesh, and that sent a chill down her. She wasn't sure if it was her heart racing, but the fairy looked at her momentarily, almost questioning her before turning back to the last few bites of the sandwich.

"My husband is not going to believe this," Naomi said, trying to catch her breath as she watched the girl eat. The fairy looked toward the door. "Where are you wounded at?" Naomi took one step forward, trying to get a better look at her as the table partially hid her. The girl held out her leg, and she could see two nasty cuts on her muscular calf. "Oh, that's bad, dear. I can bandage it for you."

The girl looked at her with curiosity and then down at her leg before returning to let their eyes meet. She then shook her head yes. Naomi went to the small bathroom, grabbed the first aid kit, and returned with it, setting it down on the table in front of her. She pulled out the rubbing alcohol. "This is going to sting." The fairy shook her head yes as if she knew it was going to hurt even before Naomi had said it. Naomi held a rag below the wound as she poured alcohol, and the girl squirmed under the intense pressure, but she didn't scream or make much of a sound outside of a gasp. Naomi cleaned the wound and put antiseptic on it before wrapping the fairy's muscular calf with a bandage. "Is that better?" Naomi questioned.

The fairy nodded her head yes.

"What can I do for your wing?" Naomi questioned as she looked from the part of the wing that was on the nearby counter and then to the girl.

The girl shook her head as she looked at the table, "Overtime, it will heal itself." Her voice was barely a whisper, but it made the hairs stand on Naomi's arm to attention. She sounded so quiet and sweet when she spoke.

"I can't believe fairies are real," Naomi said as she took a seat across the table from the fairy. The girl smiled large, giving Naomi a better look at the large canines, and this made her nervous for a different reason. Those teeth were much like the fairy's nails, meant for tearing flesh. Those two things alone told Naomi this creature was a predator, but for some reason, she didn't strike fear into her. Naomi was just completely enthralled by her appearance and the realization that fairies were real.

"What is your name?" Naomi questioned again; she hadn't gotten an answer earlier and was trying to pressure the girl too much.

"Nidaw," the fairy replied, putting her hand across her exposed chest. "I'm Nidaw."

"Nidaw, that's a beautiful name," Naomi replied. It was such an unusual name, and Naomi was sure there was some sort of meaning behind it, and she didn't have to guess what it meant. There was so much about this girl's past that she didn't know, or that there was any possible way of her knowing. And she wondered if the Nidaw knew enough of humans to answer questions to anything close to satisfaction.

"I'm Naomi," she replied. There was a sense of acknowledgment and understanding, though it shouldn't have surprised Naomi with everything she had read in the journal about Nidaw. Naomi found herself admiring the fairy's eyelashes, they were long and beautiful, and they seemed to accentuate how amazing her violet eyes were. "Are there any more"—she paused a moment—"like you out there?"

The girl looked confused for a moment before she shook her head no. It was then Naomi realized the expression wasn't confusion but an overwhelming sense of sadness.

"Are you the last…?" Naomi looked at her, trying to gauge if there was any sign of sorrow. She shook her head no in reply.

"Home," Nidaw stated.

"So there used to be a lot more of you here?" Naomi questioned.

The fairy shook her head yes. "Long ago."

"The trap you got caught in." Naomi said as she pointed to her leg. "Who set it, do you know?"

The fairy's eyes grew wide, and she placed the palm of her hand across her mouth, but Naomi heard her whisper, "Beast."

Naomi glanced at the journals and wondered just how right her husband might have been when he connected the pictures they had gotten on the cameras to that of supposed Bigfoot sightings. "Beast," the fairy whispered again, her hand slightly pulled away from her mouth.

"Is it hunting you?" Naomi questioned.

Her hand was itching. She scratched at her palm, knowing it was her nervous habit, though it was much better than biting one's fingernails. She looked back toward the door, dying to go get her husband and Growler and introduce them to the fairy. Naomi looked back at the girl in front of her, and she didn't want to take her eyes off her, especially the wings that seemed to glow and take up the entirety of the booth behind the girl. The fairy finished off the bag of chips and then took another large drink from her pop and set it in front of her. "Where are you living? In the house?" Naomi questioned.

The girl shook her head yes slightly.

"I saw your room," Naomi said, and the fairy shook her head again.

There seemed to be a reaction in the girl whenever Naomi spoke of the house, a bit of sorrow. "What's wrong?"

"Johnson," was all she said as she lowered her head in sorrow.

"I'm sorry about Mr. Johnson. I've read his journals, and it seems like he cared for you a lot, and I can tell you cared for him," Naomi stated. "I've got his journals." She reached over in the seat beside her, picked them up, and put him on the table before her. She flipped the page open to the first, the only journal they had actually gone through, to the picture of the young woman. "Is this you?" Naomi watched as the fairy reached over, grabbed the journal, slid it back to her, and nodded her head yes. Now Naomi could see the tears begin to well in the girl's eyes. There was a story there that she wanted desperately to know. But she wasn't sure how much English the young woman knew.

"Father," she said, pointing at the drawing. She pulled it close to her breasts as if to hug the paper.

"He took care of you," Naomi said through her own tears. She hadn't really thought about it till now. The fairy was naked, though it didn't seem to bother her. "I can get you a shirt," Naomi said aloud. Before she even finished the sentence, the fairy glanced down at her body. "You don't want one, do you?"

The fairy shook her head no.

Naomi smiled as she tried to make herself relax in the seat. The RV wrenched to one side violently, causing stuff to fall to the floor and making a lot of noise. Naomi had no time to react, feeling it shift in its position again and then up as if tornado-strength winds had hit against one side. It lifted into the air and flailed violently down on the side. Naomi felt the glass from the windows break as she gasped, trying to catch her breath. It all seemed to happen in a matter of a couple of seconds without warning. Naomi struggled to catch her breath. Just as she gathered herself, an appliance that had been sitting on the countertop crashed into her side, causing her to gasp out as it knocked the wind from her. A shotgun blast rang out, echoing on the inside of the toppled RV. Her ears were ringing from the shot as if it had gone off right next to her head. She placed her hand on the back of her head and instantly felt the moisture. She was bleeding. She had taken a much harder hit into the side of the wall than she had expected. Then a second shot rang out, and Naomi looked to the fairy or where she had been sitting as she heard the third shot go off outside the RV. She could hear Growler whimpering and trying to bark, but the small dog was obviously terrified, afraid of what it was seeing.

"Garrett," Naomi mumbled, worried about her husband. Naomi forced herself up into a seated position. She could see the fairy now. Her head rolled over on the counter, her eyes were shut, and she was obviously unconscious. Naomi looked for her pistol, having no clue where it had been flung to when the RV flipped. "Garrett!" she yelled out, hoping to hear her husband. There had been no more shots, and she couldn't hear anything from the ringing in her ears. "Garrett, are you okay?" She paused, trying to listen as she placed the hand on the back of her head once again, the ringing was getting worse, and her vision was getting blurry now. "Garrett, please answer me," she mumbled as she collapsed to one knee. She was struggling to breathe now on top of everything else where the air-fryer had hit her in the side. A fourth shotgun blast rang out, and she smiled. Her husband was still alive, and he would come for her. Then she heard the low rumbling growl of something else, something sinister, just before she lost consciousness.

Chapter Twelve

Garrett

Garrett opened his eyes, trying to catch his breath, but everything hurt. The last thing he remembered was leveling the shotgun and pulling the trigger. He felt like he had been black-out drunk without the drink. He couldn't remember at first what it was he had shot at; it was so large, and one minute, it was just there in front of him. It was coming to him slowly. It stood just in the firelight, breathing so heavily that it sounded like wind blowing through the trees. Its eyes leveled on the RV, and it burst into a run faster than anything its size had a right to be. Garrett was not sure exactly how many shots he got off; he only knew they didn't slow the beast down.

Garrett tried to focus. He could hear Growler somewhere nearby whimpering as he opened his eyes. The creature moved fast and with purpose as it stepped away from the fire, only for a moment leaving a clear sightline for Garrett to see Growler. There was another dog there sitting only half in the firelight, and the other half seemed to disappear into the black. Its fur was dark and spotted; it looked like an English mastiff but bigger. The thing seemed to be as tall as some adults, even though it was lying on its belly. It knocked Growler from one paw to the next and snorted at the smaller dog whenever it tried to run away, just setting its massive paw down on the puppy.

"Stop it," Garrett mumbled, trying to get the beast's attention. All he genuinely wanted was for it to leave Growler alone. "Stop it," he said again. He knew he was speaking but wasn't entirely sure any sound was coming out.

Garrett realized he was only looking through one eye. His other was matted closed from blood or mud, he couldn't quite tell. He took a deep breath as he tried to look around with his good eye. He saw his wife lying on the ground. "Naomi," he gasped out again, unsure if he made a sound looking from his wife to Growler.

Garrett knew he was suspended in the air, though he could feel twigs at his toes. He wasn't far from the ground. He hadn't realized he was naked until a cold breeze brushed across his body.

It was then he saw the other woman, remembering that Naomi had been talking to someone when he woke up. But most of all, Garrett saw her wings as they glistened in the firelight. She was naked as well, but at least his wife was still modest and covered. He again tried to focus on the large dog that tormented Growler. He could see it better now as his vision was growing clearer. The beast's leathery dark skin was littered with red freckles, and though he thought it was the fire and the pain playing tricks on him, he thought he could see slight horns coming out of the beast's massive head. It continued to swat Growler from one paw to the other. "Stop it." This time he had spoken, the large dog-like animal stopped and twisted his head to look at Garrett. The beast snarled, and even though he was nowhere close, he thought he could feel its warm breath on his skin and smell the foul stench of death. There was no doubt in Garrett's mind this hellhound-like dog he was watching toy with his dog was the beast that had left the tracks in the woods.

A large mountainous figure stepped into the light of the fire. It looked down at the large dog and grunted before stepping further into the light. It walked until it stood beside the fairy and looked at Naomi. Garrett realized what it was doing. It was looking over what it had caught. It was covered in fur that Garrett realized now was some sort of coat made up of several animals all sewn into one large overcoat, he wasn't sure, but he thought he could see human skin within the pattern. Its head was twice the size of a normal human's, a pale white, and as he shifted his head to look in the direction of Garrett, it was hard to tell where the man's head ended and his thick chest began. His eyes were deformed, one much larger than the other, and it looked like a crust was forming over the larger of them. His jaw was twisted with broken and jagged teeth, his nose was flat and white, and Garrett noticed the left side was missing a big hunk of flesh, exposing the cavity behind. The creature mumbled something as he again turned and looked at Garrett and laughed. He thought he was pointing somewhere down his abdomen, and Garrett had an uneasy feeling he knew what the gruesome creature was laughing at.

He spoke again, sounding like he had a mouth full of food. It was as much a growl as it was words. He turned back, looking at the fire as he drove a wooden spear into the ground with such force. Garrett thought he could feel the swings of the hammer from where he hung in the tree. A moment later, it circled to the other end of the fire and drove another into the ground to a similar height. The horror took Garrett, forcing him to twist against his bonds, the creature was making a spit to roast meat on, and he didn't have to guess what was on the menu.

Garrett swung and kicked, trying everything he could to get his wrists to flop free from the rope, but it wouldn't give. The beast made a noise as it shifted its frame to look at Garrett and growl. Garrett stopped when it stood up straight and approached with a knife in hand. He reached down, grabbed his wife by the back of the shirt collar, and dragged her toward the fire.

"No, you bastard!" Garrett yelled, putting all his energy into his voice, trying to make him sound much larger than he was.

The beast dropped his wife in her spot, turned to look at him, and smiled. It was a smile he would never forget; jagged and broken teeth filled the darkness of his mouth as he laughed again at Garrett.

This was an ogre. He had read many fairytales as a kid and young adult when he was growing up, but the way ogre's were often described in those tales were horrendous ugly creatures. There was no doubt in Garrett's mind he was looking at an ogre. The ogre looked from Garrett to the fairy and then focused in on Growler as the puppy was still being swatted back and forth by the bigger dog. It looked like Growler was basically lying there now, having given up on any chance of escape. Garrett continued to fight with it, grumbling against the bonds that held him in the air. The ogre reached down, grabbing the fairy by the back of its snow-white hair.

"Leave her alone, you freak!" Garrett yelled again, figuring the fairy needed just as much protection as his wife or, for that matter, everyone in the group. He would never forgive himself if he didn't at least try and save her. The ogre looked back at him with a displeased raised brow before he stood. He laughed and pointed a half finger in Garrett's direction. There was almost a chuckle roaming in the air as he took two steps toward him.

The ogre stopped in his tracks as Growler latched onto a small hanging piece of leather. Garrett hadn't even realized the bigger dog had let him go. The ogre reached down and grabbed the pup by the back of its neck, and lifted it in the air. The ogre took a smell of the animal before he tossed it back to its hellhound to play with.

Garrett struggled at the bonds slinging his legs back and forth, hoping the motion would allow him to slide free. Before he could do anything else, the beast was there, grabbing him by the throat. He pulled his head within a couple of inches of Garrett, and the smell of its breath almost made him throw up. He felt the knife enter his side, pain shooting through his entire body. He watched as the ogre pulled the knife back up to his mouth and licked the blood clear and an extra lick on his lips in appreciation of the taste. A large grin graced its face as it held the knife up, pointing the point against Garrett's chest. Garrett wanted to back away, but it wasn't possible as the tip pierced his skin. Again, the ogre laughed.

The ogre went back to the fire. It came back, grabbing at the fairy, dragging her by its hair closer to the fire. Garrett continued to struggle until the rope finally snapped. He hit the ground, feeling as if a truck had hit him, knocking him into a coughing fit from the pain. All he could hear was a thunderous roar as the ogre laughed at him. Garrett couldn't move. It all hurt so much. He lay there listening, then he felt a hot breath on the back of his neck, and he twisted just enough to look, and the mastiff-looking dog was looming over top of him. Growler circled the beast, finding his courage, and placed himself between it and Garrett. He began to growl and bark, trying to warn him off.

Garrett slowly moved his hand down the side of his body until he felt the wet sticky blood from where he'd been stabbed. He let out an audible gasp as he felt the wound and how deep it was. He glanced at his wife. Her eyes were wide open, and she was looking at him. He didn't even realize she was awake for it all. He mouthed, "I love you," forcing a smile. The smile was odd to him, but if he was going to die, the last thing he wanted to see was his beautiful wife and for her to know he loved her.

She said the same with no sound. "I love you."

Garrett pushed himself up onto his elbows. The ogre was too occupied by the fire to be paying him any attention even though he was no longer tied up. He looked around the grounds looking for anything that might be a weapon. He wasn't going to just lay there and die. He looked at the fairy. She was on her stomach as well, just like his wife. Her wings seemed to cover her like a shelter to protect her from everything though Garrett figured they didn't protect her as much as they appeared. Garrett rose onto his knees, looking down at his side wound. Then, he pushed up to one of his feet and the other, wobbling though he was in tremendous pain.

"Hey," he said out loud, and even that seemed to cause a spike in pain. Garrett grabbed a nearby stick, using it to help hold himself up to a steadying position. "Hey, ugly!" he said out loud again, trying to garner the ogre's attention.

The Ogre snorted as he looked back at Garrett. The creature stood on the side of the fire. It was twice as broad as Garrett, and his arms seemed to be as big as Garrett's own body as he took three steps toward him. Garrett was beginning to see out of his swollen eye, and he saw the ogre even more clearly now. He had to look up at the creature as he took a step back. As the ogre stepped forward, it seemed to blot out the firelight with his size. He could see the ogre's upper body now, and there were buckshot spots still peppering the upper torso where Garrett had shot him. It may not have done much damage to him, but it brought a smile to Garrett, even just the idea that he got a few shots off on it. Garrett struck with the large piece of wood. The wood splintered and shattered on the ogre's forearm. He didn't see the other arm hump forward and hit flat-palmed, knocking Garrett backward at least four feet onto his back. Garrett knew that hit broke some ribs. His entire body ached from the pressure on his chest.

Garrett rolled over onto his side, looking back in the direction of the fire where the ogre returned, stacking more wood to the flames. Garrett struggled to get to his feet again, returning to his search for weapons. Garrett didn't see any weapons, but he did see an opportunity. He looked at his wife and then at the fairy and whispered, "Run."

Garrett shifted back up onto his knees. He ran through the middle of the camp, knowing he would catch both large predator's attention, but that was what he wanted. Even as he entered the darkness, he yelled, "Come and get me!"

There was a moment he wondered why he didn't hear anything chasing him. All he could see was black. He knew which way he was going, the direction of the end of the property, but more importantly, he was running toward the treehouse. Maybe he'd be safe if he got to the tree and up in it. He heard something coming through the brush giving chase, the mastiff-like dog, but he could hear the faint sound of something grunting coming up after it. They were both chasing him, and he smiled, knowing his plan had worked. Maybe his wife would get away even if he did not. It wasn't the speed he was running that was bothering him; it was going as fast as he could barefoot. He felt something cut into his foot, imagining a rock on the edge of the stream as he turned, following it, knowing the treehouse was waiting near a waterfall. He just hoped it would be easy to find once he got there. He kept running as far and as fast as he could. He could hear the animal gaining on him, even over the sound of him running. He gasped, imagining he was no more than a hundred yards from the tree. With safety almost in sight, he turned back, looking in the direction he'd fled. He could hardly see anything even though the moon was high and full, but it was hard to see in the trees with so many leaves still on them.

Garrett took a deep breath as he turned and started running again. And for a moment, he allowed himself to think he was going to make it as he tried to pace himself, but more importantly, he didn't want to fall flat on his face and get caught that way. He'd surveyed the property twice; once the other day after his wife had told him about the tree houses, he'd come and inspected them. So he knew just about where it was he was going, but mostly he was just following the stream as the moon seemed to reflect off the water. He stopped for a moment, but all he could hear was the roar of something cutting through the brush after him. He could hear a growl coming up behind him. He realized it was not the massive dog but the ogre. Garrett took a couple of steps back and then felt the warm breeze on the back of his neck, realizing he wasn't going to make it to the tree house. Garrett turned slowly; the mastiff struck at him with its large claws across his chest. The force of the blow was enough to knock him back onto his back. Just as he sat up to look at his wound, the ogre was standing above him. The ogre smiled its rotten smile, and it was obvious to Garrett the beast enjoyed the chase. Even though it had a tough time catching its breath as it looked down on him. The ogre pointed at him with its half finger and looked at the mastiff.

"Up," the ogre said. Its jaw opened as drool dripped from its mouth down onto Garrett. Growler stepped up between them, growling. The ogre reached down, picked up the small dog, and gave it a curious look before it laughed. The mastiff growled, and Garrett looked at the big dog, realizing it was looking up at the ogre with a jealous look in its eyes. Garrett took off, ignoring the pain that seemed to originate everywhere. He wasn't sure anymore which of his wounds hurt the worst or if maybe he was going into shock. He remembered the axe sitting at the base of the tree. It was a chance for him to not only get away but defend himself. He could see the form of the tree house in the distance. All he had to do was make it there. He kept running. He could hear it now, the bigger dog coming up behind him, no longer trying to be quiet as he approached. He reached the tree, grabbed the axe, and turned to face the animal. He barely had any time to react. The mastiff leaped through the darkness with its mouth wide. Garrett sidestepped and swung the axe downward from his shoulder with all the force he could summon.

Garrett opened his eyes, looking at the severed head of the hellhound, and smiled just as the ogre appeared through the woods to them. The ogre looked confused from Garrett to the mastiff before he rushed forward to its pet. Garret slipped past him, grabbing Growler on the run. Garrett wasn't far from the tree house when the ogre bellowed out a scream of agony from losing its pet.

Garrett seemed to get back to the other camp where he had left his wife and the fairy quicker than he had in getting to the treehouse. He stood catching his breath, Growler still held in his arms. His wife and the fairy were gone. He smiled as he took back into a run in the direction of home. He was probably only a hundred feet from the ogre's camp when he saw his wife with the fairy over her shoulder carrying her.

"You're alive," Naomi said, turning to look at him. Garrett tried his best to ignore his wounds as he took the fairy from her, flipping her over his shoulder. "We've got to get out of here, get to the truck, and call in the army or something," Garrett glanced back the way he had come.

"You're hurt," Naomi said, placing a hand on his chest.

"We've got to go," Garrett said as he took a deep breath and started walking. He only made it about a hundred yards before the effects of the wounds and his bare feet caught up with him, and he toppled over, rolling onto his back. In the process, the fairy landed on top of him.

Garrett grinned through the pain. "Take her," he mumbled, pushing up into a seated position. "I'll be right behind you."

Naomi looked at him, confused. "I'm not leaving you."

"You have to. Soon as I catch my breath, I'll catch you, and I'll carry her again, but you need to go," Garrett was struggling to breathe. "I love you."

"I love you," Naomi grumbled to herself as she put the fairy onto her shoulder.

Garrett rolled over onto his stomach coughing up blood. Growler ran up to him as if to encourage him to get up. "Go, Growler, protect them." Growler twisted its head to one side before it whimpered, giving Garrett a long, pity-filled look. "Go," Garrett said no more as Growler ran off to catch Naomi. Garrett looked, he could no longer see Naomi and the fairy, and it was only a moment later, Growler was also gone from sight. He rolled over to his back, coughing up more blood.

#

Naomi

Naomi wasn't sure how far she had gone after leaving her husband. Growler had overtaken them and was going back and forth, trying to get her to hurry. Despite the fairy's small frame, she was getting heavy, and her legs were weak. She dropped to one knee, trying her best to cradle the woman on her shoulder.

"Are you okay?" she questioned.

She could barely tell the woman was even breathing. It was then Growler came back into the opening growling, looking back into the darkness, and Naomi feared he wasn't growling at her husband. The pup growled and bounced in its steps, trying to encourage them to go on. Naomi stood, pulling the girl back up onto her shoulders, and started moving again. She moved a hundred feet when she found herself again leaning against a tree. This time she thought she could see the outline of the RV in the distance. She took a deep breath and moved a dozen steps more, and she could see the light from the fire still burning. Then it hit her. She could hear nothing coming from behind her. Her husband wasn't coming. She looked back for a moment, hearing Growler again urging her on.

"I'm coming," she turned, looking at Growler. She positioned the fairy back on her shoulder and steadied herself. She started this time she didn't stop; she could feel the heat on her face. Naomi collapsed so close to the fire she could reach out and grab it. She huffed, trying to catch her breath. She never thought she'd make it this far. Growler was standing beside her, licking her face with encouragement. She looked back at the fairy, whose eyes were now open, staring at her coldly. She heard the rumbling sound coming through the woods behind them now. She hadn't heard it before over her own movement. But it was coming. She grabbed a nearby log that was in the flame and turned to hold the fire torch out in the direction of the sound. The beast appeared from the darkness, huffing each labored breath it took, and Naomi thought she could see tears on its face. She didn't have to wonder about the hellhound. She knew her husband had successfully killed it when he had come to help them and not the snarling beast.

The ogre stopped when it got so close to the flame with the torch that she could almost stab its face with it. It grumbled as it showed its teeth and smiled.

"Mine," it pointed at the fairy. "Mine all mine, mine, mine," it repeated so many times she didn't know how many times it said it. The sound of its voice sent a chill down her back. She knew she couldn't just hand the fairy over; the ogre intended to eat her. Naomi stepped forward, pushing the torch forward with her. She imagined it was burning any hairs that were left of the rough skin of the ogre, but it never so much as flinched as it reached a meaty hand out, grabbing the flame and pushing it aside, again pointing at the fairy and repeating, "Mine."

Naomi was sure her husband wasn't coming, and there was no way she could let the ogre have her. She moved the flame away from the ogre and took three steps forward, so close now she could smell his rotten breath. "Mine." She pointed at the fairy and stomped her foot, not taking her eyes off the ogre.

"Mine, mine," it said again as it lowered its face. Naomi wanted to puke when she got a good smell of its breath as she glared into its eyes.

"No," Naomi proclaimed, stomping her foot again and pointing her arm straight at the fairy.

The ogre stood straight, looking confused about what had just happened. It looked at the fairy and then looked at Naomi, and she could see as it gritted its teeth and snarled. "She is mine," Naomi said again, trying to put more baritone in her voice. Naomi again took a step forward and leaned a little as if a toddler throwing a tantrum. "Mine, mine."

She looked to the fairy, who was watching her now with a slight smile on her lips. Naomi again focused on the ogre, but it was smiling, and she realized he had called her bluff. The beast grabbed Naomi by her shoulder, pulled her closer, and opened its mouth as if it would bite her. Suddenly there was a jolt, and she opened her eyes. The fairy was on the ogre's shoulder with her enlarged canines ripping into the soft of his neck. It recoiled in pain, dropping Naomi in the motion. The ogre yelled out in pain.

Naomi reached down, grabbed the torch, and circled around to get behind the ogre just as he slung the fairy off to one side. She put the torch to the seasoned fur on its back, and it instantly caught fire. She took a step back, looking for weapons. The pistol that had been sitting on the table before the RV had been flipped. She saw it sitting on the ground not far from the fire. Naomi turned to face them. The fairy was again on top of the ogre, slashing out with its claws. The ogre grabbed her, tossing her into the darkness. She shot twice, hitting it in the back. She saw Garrett hobbling into the firelight now. She released a sigh of relief, happy to see he was still alive. The ogre turned, knocking Garrett back to the ground, and he'd moved after he hit the unforgiving surface. Naomi picked up the shotgun at her feet, turning her attention to the ogre trying to draw it from her injured husband. She shot it twice, neither time phasing the large monster. The third time she pulled the trigger, it only clicked. It was empty. The fairy appeared from the darkness, grabbed the nearby axe and brought it down into the ogre's chest, and it bellowed out in pain. And then just stopped and looked down at her and laughed. It reached, grabbing her by her waist. "Mine," it had said again, opening its mouth giving Naomi a side eye look of pleasure.

Naomi wrenched a shell into the shotgun she had found on the ground. She quickly circled around to the ogre before he could bite the fairy, who was lashing out and striking, trying to get out of its grip. Naomi shoved the end of the shotgun into the ogre's mouth and pulled the trigger. It recoiled, dropping the fairy in the process. She reached down, helping the fairy to her feet. The ogre was still alive, sitting on its hands and knees but slowly crawling away from them. She turned to look at her husband, who was trying to get up. Once he steadied himself, he picked up the axe and approached the ogre. The first hit cut its left hand off at the palm. It rose, looking at its missing fingers still on the ground in front of it.

The large beast just looked as its eyebrow raised and started laughing as it looked at Garrett. It swung its remaining hand quickly in his direction. Naomi pulled the trigger. There was a moment where they all four stood silent and still as the ogre looked at the bloodied stump of its remaining hand.

Naomi and Garrett watched as the ogre looked at the fairy who was standing in the firelight, her wings shining and glowing in the light. Naomi reached the ground, picking up another shell as she limped around to face the ogre, who continued looking at the fairy.

"Hey," she said, and it turned its attention back to her. She pulled the trigger, the barrel so close to the ogre's one good eye it ripped through the back of its skull, and there was no doubt it was dead now. "Mine."

<u>*Epilogue*</u>

Growler

The sound of the two roosters making their wake-up call roused him from his slumber. The heat from the fireplace felt nice. He kicked the blanket off him, moved over to the door, and popped his head out the small magnetic door allowing him to come and go as he pleased. The cabin had been done for months, though he didn't really have a grasp on how long it had been. The leaves on the trees were starting to change colors once again, much like they were changing when they first moved here so long ago.

He moved to the edge of the gravel road giving a last glance at their home. He was so glad the strangers who built it were gone. It had been a few months of too many unfamiliar scents through the heat of the summer when the strange men had been there building it. Growler wasn't alone. Dad was on edge the entire time they were here, and Mom had spent all her time at the waterfall with the girl with the wings. Growler knew they were worried about the girl; she was family now, and Growler would protect her the same as anyone he saw as family.

He especially enjoyed it when she would scratch him behind his ears. Her claws were sharper than Mom's or Dad's, and she dug just right at his skin.

Growler came to a sliding stop near the fence; the four goats came bouncing in his direction just as they came to greet him every morning when he went on his journey. Bruce, the large solid white dog who was placed in the pen to keep the chickens and goats safe from the coyotes and other predators, came lumbering toward Growler. Bruce was almost twice the size of Growler and had a very distinctive deep bark that even if the family was in the house, they would be woken by his bellow. He had often woken them up in the middle of the night, causing Dad to go outside with a gun to help run off intruders. Bruce slept inside with the goats and horses on most nights. Bruce came up beside the fence and trotted alongside Growler until he was on his way up the trail. The moment Growler knew he was out of sight, the other dog bellowed out his bark.

He reached the outside perimeter of the property. He heard Bones coming up behind him. Bones was always late, but Growler knew he was still just a puppy, but he always caught up about the time Growler reached the fence. Bones was solid black and had sharp features, and he was already about Growler's size despite only being here a little while. Growler was starting to realize that of the three, Bones, Bruce, and himself, he was going to be the smallest of the three. And though he suspected Bruce was older, Bruce had his set job. It was up to Growler to watch over everyone else here, and he had to keep Bones in line, who often got distracted by any little thing.

Bones kept pace as they ran the fence along, not until they came to the well-worn trail leading to where they would get a drink. They never stopped until they reached the waterfall.

The girl with the wings was waiting for them when they rushed down the trail coming to a sliding stop at the edge of the water. She was smiling and laughing at them as she often did. Mom and Dad left treats with her that she was always more than generous with. Most of all, she was there waiting to scratch him behind the ears. They would spend a while here, Growler often felt like Mom and Dad wanted her protected above all else, so they never complained about him spending too much time here. Often it would be Mom who would find them here.

Bones had a very distinctive howl when he was distressed. It broke Growler from enjoying his ear scratches, and he jolted up. Both he and the winged girl looked in the direction Bones had wandered. Growler looked at her, and she only smiled as he jolted off into the wilderness.

Growler hurriedly charged off, following the sound of Bones' multiple howls. He broke into the clearing where Bones stood, his nose to the ground, circling the clearing. Growler paced forward, only stopping when he caught the unfamiliar scent that caused Bones to panic. His own heart raced; it was the distinct smell of decay as he lifted his head to look around. No one was there watching, but he could feel the eyes on him as a couple of the black feathered birds landed on a nearby tree and cawed. A beast had been nearby.

About the Author:

Steven Paul Watson is many things: a writer, artist, amateur photographer, and avid outdoorsman as well as an all-around geek. His love of writing includes soul-chilling science fiction, fantasy, all things supernatural/horror, and a passion for steampunk/alternate reality.

In his free time spends a lot of time out in nature hiking the hills near his home. There is no better way to stroke one's imagination than being outdoors in the wilderness having real adventures that feed the ones he puts on a page. Steven is also an avid crafter and artist making a lot of jewelry and woodcrafts. Loves dogs and spending time with his family.